This is a photo of Marco, looking super worried. Notice his hands are all clenched up like a cute baby koala, and his eyes are all like "Whoaaa!" Adorbs.

Wha? I wasn't scared . . . look at you! You look horrified!

Uhhh . . . that's my "concentrating on doing awesome magic" face. You know that.

DISNEP

STAR
VS THE FORCES OF EVIL

Star *and* Marco's
Guide to
Mastering Every Dimension

written by

Star Butterfly *and* Marco Diaz

With help from Dominic Bisignano, Amber Benson,
Devin Taylor, and Cindy Plourde

Based on the series created by Daron Nefcy

DISNEP PRESS

Los Angeles • New York

Copyright © 2017 Disney Enterprises, Inc.

Design by Lindsay Broderick

A very special thank-you to Andrea Atencio, Drake Brodahl, Tatiana Bull, Becky Dreistadt Alison Donato, Eric Gonzalez, Britta Reitman, and Anna States for all their help in making this book happen.

For information address Disney Press,
1101 Flower Street, Glendale, California 91201.

Printed in the United States of America
First Hardcover Edition, March 2017
1 3 5 7 9 10 8 6 4 2

FAC-008598-17027
ISBN 978-1-4847-7419-9

Library of Congress Control Number: 2016953973

For more Disney Press fun,
visit www.disneybooks.com
Visit DisneyChannel.com

SUSTAINABLE FORESTRY INITIATIVE   Certified Sourcing
www.sfiprogram.org
SFI-00993
Logo Applies to Text Stock Only

A Public Service Announcement from Your Authoress, <u>Star Butterfly</u>

I wanted to take a moment to tell you about something very important. It's what made me decide on the spur of the moment to write this book (besides wanting to share my—our—knowledge with everyone in **every** dimension).

And to drag your friends into writing it when they're supposed to be at the dojo practicing karate!

After many seconds of thought, I have vowed—as me is my witness—with this book to banish the greatest evil in the universe:

BOREDOM.

Join me on my journey to combat boredom in all its forms. The adventure begins when you turn the page!

<u>THIS ONE?</u>

Great, we're just getting started and we already lost Pony Head.

Contents

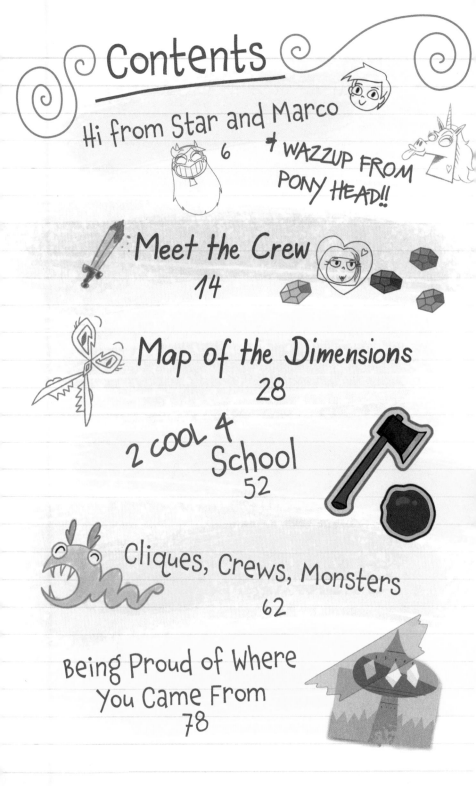

Star Butterfly

Hi! I'm Star Butterfly, princess of Mewni! Today I'm bored, and I can't take it, so me and my best friend, Marco, are gonna create a secret guide to everything you need to know about everything important in the multiverse etc., but shhhhh . . . don't tell my parents.

YOUR BEST FRIEND? RU KIDDING ME, B?

Wait . . . why am I being included?

Marco, you'll get your chance in a sec. And who knows, maybe someday our guidebook will end up on display in the Mewniseum! Anyway, when I write it looks like this,

when Marco writes it looks like this,

AND THIS IS ME, PRINCE$$ PONY HEAD!!!

By Marco

6

Five Facts You Didn't Know about Star, by Marco Diaz

1. She likes to walk on Bubble Wrap. POP!

2. Her favorite Earth food is honeydew boba tea. POP!

3. She's scared of the Easter bunny. Wouldn't YOU be?

4. She's a great whistler.

5. She forgets the Pythagorean theorem but remembers your friendiversary.

6. HER BE$T BESTIE IS PONY HEAD.

FIVE THINGS MARCO IS SO ANNOYING ABOUT (LIKE HE KNOWS EVERYTHING OHMYGOODNE$$)

1. OKAY, FIRST OF ALL, LIKE, YOU DON'T KNOW EVERYTHING

2. ABOUT STAR CUZ, LIKE, YOU'RE SECOND BESTIES, 'KAY?

3. AND SECOND OF ALL, FIRST BESTIES KNOW WAY MORE THAN SECOND BESTIES.

This isn't a list.

4. STOP MAKING RULES! OTHER PEOPLE FROM OTHER CULTURES HAVE DIFFERENT KINDS OF LISTS, OKAY, AND THIS IS HOW WE MAKE A LIST IN MY CULTURE.

5. STAR, YOU'RE MY BESTIE, GIRL! Awwwwwww!

Marco Diaz

Hi, I'm Marco Diaz, only child. Star Butterfly's my best friend. I guess I'm supposed to say hi... Wait, why are we doing this again?

Because I'm bored and because you're my best friend!

Okay, yeah, I guess so.

What am I supposed to say here?

Well, maybe talk about Earth? Write what ya know, ya know? And you can help me remember stuff. Like give me notes on my notes, yeah?

Well, I mean, I was born here. I think if anyone (between me and Star) knows about Earth, it's me. Well, Earth is roundish . . . third planet from the sun. . . .

No, Marco, not that stuff . . . like interesting things . . . but you don't need to say it all now. We have a lot of writing to do. Why did you ask me to help, then?

Five Facts You Didn't Know about Marco Diaz, by Star Butterfly

1. His favorite drink is hot chocolate with cinnamon in it.
   2. He's saving money to buy a canoe.
   3. He likes board games.
   4. He plays "jazz piano."

Why did you put that in quotes?

5. His middle name is Ubaldo, making his initials M.U.D.

JUST BRUTAL. Hey!

6. & 7. HE'S B-FLY'S SECOND BESTIE. WE CALL HIM EARTHTURD 4 SHORTz.

This says FIVE facts about me, and those are not facts.

Five Things Marco Can't Stand, by Marco Diaz

1. Jam bands
2. The words <u>tasty</u> and <u>mucus</u>
3. People who take pictures of their lunch
4. Pictures of people's lunch
5. The name Ubaldo *Ditto.*

Marco's Super Awesome Nachos!

Wait . . . I can say that because it's my middle name. . . . If you say that it's just mean.

9

PRINCESS PONY HEAD

OMG, I CAN'T BELIEVE THAT U PUT ME IN LAST!

We didn't put you in at all. . . . You put yourself in.

I WASN'T TALKING TO YOU, EARTHTURD!

Guys . . . no fighting. . . . This is a guide to the multiverse. . . . It's supposed to be helpful!

UGH . . . N.E.WAYZ. MY NAME IS PRINCE$$ PONY HEAD OF THE PONY HEADS.

DON'T ASK ABOUT MY LEGS. . . . ASK ABOUT MY PARTIES. OH! SPEAKING OF, OMG, DID YOU KNOW DJ JUMP-JUMP IS DOING A SET AT THE BOUNCE LOUNGE 2-NITE? :O IT'S GONNA BE OFF THA HOOK! I GOTTA GO . . . ON THE MOVE . . . 2 COOL 4 SCHOOL. . . .

HOW WELL DO YOU KNOW YOUR BESTIE?

A MAGAZINE-STYLE POP QUIZ I MADE UP ABOUT ME!

1. WHAT IS MY FAVE PLACE TO DO SOME DANCING DAMAGE?

   A. ST. OLGA'S REFORM SCHOOL FOR WAYWARD PRINCESSES

   B. QUEST BUY

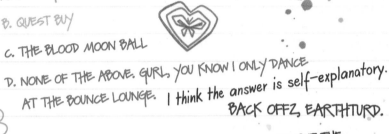

   C. THE BLOOD MOON BALL

   D. NONE OF THE ABOVE. GURL, YOU KNOW I ONLY DANCE
     AT THE BOUNCE LOUNGE. *I think the answer is self-explanatory.*
                             BACK OFFZ, EARTHTURD.

2. SPEAKING OF EARTHTURD, IF YOU HAVE A SECOND BESTIE BUT THE
REAL FIRST BESTIE YOU HAVE COMES TO VISIT, YOU SHOULD:

   A. NOT BE AFRAID TO DISAPPOINT A SECOND BESTIE. I MEAN,
     C'MON, THEY'RE SECOND—DO THE MATH.

   B. BY DISAPPOINT I MEAN IT'S FINE TO GO AHEAD AND
     BACK-BURNER SECOND BESTIE.

   C. LOOK AT SECOND BESTIE'S CLOTHES AND BE LIKE, "IS THIS
     A PERSON I WANT TO GO OUT WITH . . . A PERSON IN A RED
     HOODIE?" NO OFFENSE. *That's not how that works. . . . You don't get*
                          to pretend something's not offensive just
                        because you say "no offense" afterward.

3. HOW DID B-FLY GET ME MY BIRTHDAY GROOVE BACK?

   A. B-FLY MADE ME GROOVY BIRTHDAY CUPCAKES.

   B. B-FLY BROKE INTO ST. O'S TO SAVE ME.

   C. B-FLY REVERSED THE BRAINWASHING MISS HEINOUS TRIED TO GIVE ME.

   D. ALL OF THE ABOVE—CUZ B-FLY IS MY BESTIE!

     It's D—and I helped, too, remember? WHATEVZ.

Friendship: Three's a Crowd

How to Deal When Your Bestie's ^SECOND Bestie Brings Conflict to the Table

When you sit down at the potluck dinner of friendship, sometimes someone will bring a Crock-Pot full of negativity that's so bitter it ruins your platter of super-awesome nachos.

I actually like Princess Pony Head. *O I C U TRYIN' 2 GET ON MY GOOD SIDE. . . .* Sure, at first she was kinda mean and kinda rude and maybe she tried to kill me . . . but she's gotten nicer. . . . Well, a little bit nicer. But she's Star's best friend from Mewni and that means I have to deal even when she *BUT ALSO IN TH UNIVERSE, TOO, AS WELL, ALSO* calls me Earthturd . . . which is not who I feel like I am as a person. My mom took me to a Spirit Realization Workshop at the community college, and after the evaluation they said that I was a Number Seven—a quiet warrior of peace and perseverance.

So, clearly science doesn't back up what Pony Head says about me. *ARE U SURE THIS ISN'T A ROLE-PLAYING GAME?*

MARCO DIAZ   **7**

Quiet warrior of peace
and perseverance.

Attributes

7
- Meanness: -3
- Positivity: +3
- Karate: Amazing

I also learned in workshop
that it's best to resolve conflict
through positivity—essentially,
kill 'em with kindness. So I try
to think of nice things to say
about Pony Head when there's
conflict. When she makes fun of
my pants, I try to point out how
she makes having no legs work
to her advantage, and how I'm
jealous she doesn't have to
make a pants decision each morning like I do.

AWWWW, THANKS, MARCO . . . HONESTLY, YOU DO LOOK
GOOD IN SKINNY JEANS, BABY GIRL. BUT THEN, EVERYONE
LOOKS GOOD IN SKINNY JEANS.

Sometimes Pony Head lies. Wait . . . no, I mean, sometimes
she tells the truth, but USUALLY she lies. In workshop we call
someone who lies a <u>liar</u>. They taught us that a liar is a Number
Three—a cloaked wizard of darkness and cowardice. Because
I am a Seven and she's a Three, in conflict we're a 7/3, which
is the fractional conflict number of friendship. I learned that
rolling a seventeen or above will resolve the conflict in my
favor, but a sixteen or lower will resolve in hers.

OKAY, MARCO, THIS IS A ROLE-PLAYING GAME.

Meet the Crew

Janna Banana

Janna's the best.
She's into witchy
stuff, which isn't
exactly what I
do, but she thinks it's the
same, so I don't wanna rain on her carnival.

No, it's "parade." Rain on her parade.

ANYWAY . . . sometimes I come home from
school and she's already there, eating our food,
which just goes to show you how at home she
feels at the Diazes'. *Oh, boy.*

She likes black magic, daggers, dead-clown
séances, the night, "street wizards," and the color
pink. She battles the patriarchy, loves to eat,
and once dated a talking skeleton.

our food

Here's the picture!

She also flirts with me and makes creepy comments about calling her after my divorce.

Oh, Marco, it sounds like you're maybe a bit jealous of her real crush, nineteenth-century poet John Keats.

I have no idea what to say to that.

Janna's spirit animal is a snake eating its own tail.

Janna's Top Tips for Chillaxing with the Occult

1. Take every opportunity you can to raise the dead—because we all know they're not gonna raise themselves. (And if you find a dead guy who does, marry him! He's a keeper!)

2. Make every séance count by really getting to know your spirit guide. They're not just guides. They're ghosts who could become poltergeists if you're not nice to them—but that could be all right, too, ya know?

3. Sometimes graves are for sleeping. Practice for the "big sleep" by enjoying all the little sleeps in a hole in the ground.

Tom Lucitor

Tom's the prince of the underworld and son of the Big Guy. He's got some anger issues I couldn't get past. . . . It's really a lot to get into, but we broke up and he won't take no for an answer. Since we're both royalty, there's sorta this pressure for us to be together, but I want to take my time. Besides, I don't know what I want, ya know? Sometimes I can't tell if he's hot or if I just think that because of all the fire. One time I broke open this box of lost souls in his bedroom and one of the souls flew up my nose and I talked backwards and crawled around like a crab for about eight hours until it went away. LOLLERSKATES. :)

Tom's Favorite Ways to Chill

1. Rigorous exorcise
2. Crushing Marco at ping-pong **He cheats!**
3. Having minions do his bidding
4. Listening to "Love Sentence" on his vintage five-disc CD player ← **I can confirm this. . . . I've seen it in action.**

Tom's spirit animal is a white tiger.

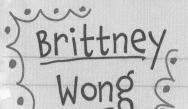

Brittney may be head
cheerleader, but when I
booby-trapped the football
field, she was pretty
unprepared to be eaten by

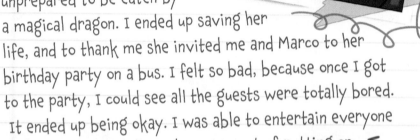

a magical dragon. I ended up saving her
life, and to thank me she invited me and Marco to her
birthday party on a bus. I felt so bad, because once I got
to the party, I could see all the guests were totally bored.
It ended up being okay. I was able to entertain everyone
and save Brittney the embarrassment of putting on
a crummy party. I guess she sorta owes
me, but who's keeping track? Ya know,
it's like I always say—pay it forward.

↖ You
destroyed
the party
bus.

  Brittney's personal magic number is one.
Which is a perfect fit, because I always hear her whispering
"I'm number one" under her breath when she's walking down
the hall at school. And there is only one of her. So I guess it's a
pretty good mantra.

  Brittney's spirit animal is a flying pig.

Brittney's Favorite After-School Activities

1. Doing karaoke alone in her room in front of her mirror ✿

2. Choreographing booty-shakin' dance moves for the
cheerleading team ✿

3. Chairing the spirit committee with an iron fist ✿

Jackie-Lynn Thomas

Jackie's pretty rad. She's easygoing and surprisingly alert for someone who looks like she just woke up. I'd hang out with her more if Marco wasn't so nervous around her. **Hey!**

Well, she is your crush. **No big secret there. :)**

Remember the time she came to our house for a sleepover and you told everyone how she was your crush to keep that demon box thingy from killing us? *Sigh.*

She skates, and she knows a lot about history.

So I broke her skateboard! Why do you have to keep bringing it up?

Three Reasons Why Jackie-Lynn Is Supercool

1. She has an awesome blue streak in her hair.

2. She only shops at charity thrift stores with the word "salvation" in their names. *It's her way of giving back.*

3. The blue streak in her hair is natural.

Jackie-Lynn's spirit animal is a basketful of kittens.

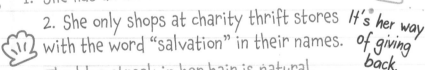

Oskar Greason

I can barely get words out to describe my feelings for Osk ♥ r. Sometimes, when the wind is just so, his hair blows back from his eyes and I can see the soul of a tortured artist behind them. He's got a record. He also makes music. He converted his car into a live/work space to take his music career on the road. One of his songs is called "Wish upon a Car," and I think it's secretly about me, but he's such a sensitive soul that he doesn't wanna reveal his true feelings.

Osk ♥ r's L ♥ ves

1. Meatball subs with chips, 'cause they're extra crunchy
2. Gene the ferret
3. Making music in his car
4. Me, Star Butterfly (A girl can dream.)
5. His keytar

Oskar's Top Three Band Names

1. Mysterious Sonograms
2. Oratory Opocalypse
3. Solitary Instructions

If Oskar was an animal, he'd be a sloth.

19

Glossaryck

Ohhhh, Glossaryck. So much to say about this little blue magic man about whom I know so little . . . about.
Grammar check.

Glossaryck lives in my family spell book. Actually, I am not sure he's technically <u>alive</u>, but he does something in there. According to my mom, he's supposed to "train" me, but I never quite experienced that. He usually just eats, confuses me, eats, makes Marco mad, eats, then sleeps. *Looks about right.*

According to my family history, he's "trained" all the queens of Mewni, going back as far as they have recorded. I guess that makes him super old. He always has cheese-curl fingers, so there are these orange spots all over my spell book.

Are you gonna say the thing?
What thing?

About how Ludo stole your book and Glossaryck went with it?

No one wants to hear about that! Hehehehe . . . But yeah, he's gone. . . . My mom's gonna get him back. Still, no matter how weird he was, everything he did seemed to be for a reason. I wonder whether or not there's a reason he's gone now.

CORNRITOS

Seven Fancy Things You Didn't Know about Glossaryck

1. He has three sisters and one brother: Tableaucontenta, Indexica, Chapterra, and Footnotryck.

2. His search for the perfect chip has led him to open 4,787,901 bags of Cornitos.

3. He sleeps in my spell book, which sort of makes it a bed, which sorta makes it gross.

4. He's trained all the queens of Mewni, but he says I'M his favorite student. :)

5. His favorite flavor of pudding is peanut butter banana.

6. He sleeps with a camouflage woobie named Fred.

7. Most of these probably aren't true, because he never tells me anything about himself.

Miss Skullnick

Skullzy teaches math at Echo Creek Academy, which is not to say I have learned any math. When I first met her, she was just a math teacher lady, but I inbettered her life by converting her into a math teacher troll lady. You could look at it like, "I turned her into a troll," but I like to say "I turned her ON to a troll!" Look, she's better off as a troll, okay . . . sheesh.

Not a word, Star.

Whatever helps you sleep at night. . . .

Three Things Trolls Have in Common with Strip Mall Dojos

1. They both smell like feet. *What?*

2. They both eat children. *What?!*

3. They both steal your money and give you nothing back in return. *That's not true! I got my red belt from a strip mall dojo!*

No, Marco, you got your red belt from a video store.

Sensei

Hey, Marco, does Sensei have a name?

Yeah, it's Sensei.

I thought "sensei" was Japanese for "teacher."

No, "sensei" means "person born before another."

So then his name is not Sensei?

We call him Sensei out of respect.

But, I mean, he learned karate from some videotapes. *So?*

So, I mean, why not just call him Cody?

Because his name is Brantley.

Three Things Marco and Sensei Have in Common

1. They both graduated middle school.

2. They are both red belts.

3. Neither of them has a driver's license.

Alfonzo and Ferguson

When I met these . . . uh . . . two guys, it was when I first arrived in Echo Creek, and they

each . . . uh . . . separately had their own charming and awkward way of welcoming me. At first I confused them for each other, but then I realized Ferguson is the one with the face on his stomach and Alfonzo is the one with the glasses.

And then they got turned into a centaur. AND it's not my fault. Well, technically it's my fault, because they were "combined" on a field trip that I took them on, but I didn't force them to become one. You can lead a centaur to water but you can't make him mutate into an Alfonzo/Ferguson/horse-thing. I <u>did</u>, however, separate them. It just got to be too weird. Thing is, now they keep asking me to put them back together.

GETTING TO KNOW YOUR NEIGHBOR THE CENTAUR

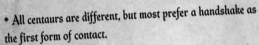

If you encounter a centaur in the wild, you might be confused. Do you shake his hand like a man, or do you rub his nose like a horse? Let's get the facts so that when you encounter a centaur, you can avoid any awkward cultural misunderstandings.

- All centaurs are different, but most prefer a handshake as the first form of contact.

- However, when approaching a centaur from behind, touch him above the tail, then walk toward his head with your hand brushing along the side of his body so he knows you are coming.

- If a centaur you've previously met doesn't seem to recognize you, he may ask to smell your breath. Don't be offended by this; a centaur's memories are strongly linked to his sense of smell. It's important to comply with his request, so just blow into his nose. Otherwise, if he sees you as a stranger, he may trample you and seize any children or gems you have with you and keep them for his own.

- Not sure what to bring to a centaur party? You should feel comfortable bringing a simple side dish. An oat and carrot casserole is best. Avoid anything with gelatin, as gelatin is commonly made from horse hooves and is seen as a distasteful item to serve to a centaur. Obviously.

- A centaur's bathroom won't have some of the finery you may be accustomed to in your castle. Often, the bathroom in a centaur's home will just be a stone room with hay on the floor. You may see this and think, "This is sort of like all the other rooms in this centaur's house." Not exactly. The hay on the floor in a centaur's bathroom is not like the furniture hay in his living room. It is actually straw, and it's meant for exactly what you think it's meant for . . . so do your business quickly and try to leave the room as you found it.

You know, now that I've read this, I'm even more convinced that separating them was the right thing to do.

Well, the right thing would have been to keep them from becoming a centaur. :)
Point Marco!

Jeremy Birnbaum

Well, what to say about Jeremy here?

Oh, allow me! Jeremy is a really snotty little brat who thinks he's better than everyone because his parents buy him whatever he wants.

He's eight years old, Marco.

And he cheats at the dojo!

Sorta how you cheated when you fought him with your monster arm? *That was different!*

Hmmmm . . .

Doesn't matter! He's a jerk and he ruins my karate time with Sensei!

Jeremy's spirit animal is ~~a koa~~ 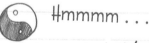 Money can't buy you a spirit animal, Jeremy.

Fun fact: Jeremy hates groundhogs because they remind him of his own fear of shadows.

Kelly
(and Sometimes Tad When They Haven't Broken Up)

Kelly (and sometimes Tad when they haven't broken up) is (are?) one of my best friends from my club days at the Bounce Lounge. Tad is her on-and-off boyfriend, who fits perfectly into her hair . . . or maybe he is her hair? I'm not always sure where one ends and the other begins. . . . I guess that means it's true love? ¯_(⊙_☉)_/¯

Star and Marco's AND PONY HEAD's Map of the Dimensions

PLAINS OF TIME

Father Time keeps time in motion by treadmilling on the Wheel of Progress, except when I freeze time and Father Time rolls around in the mud. The Plains of Time are inhabited by giant versions of pet-store animals, and lots and lots of mud. You can become a grandma or a baby or a grandma-baby if you're not careful hopscotching across the timepiece floaters on the Pocketwatch Rapids. The Memoratorium has displays of all the memories you've ever had, so it's a good idea to keep your memories clean. ;)

The Plains of Time are where I learned that using "the nod" technique doesn't get you the girl . . . and that watching yourself be lame on about a thousand television screens can be confidence boosting in a weird opposite–day kind of way.

THE BOUNCE LOUNGE

My favorite place to cheeeeee-ill. It's where all the cool cats go to hang out. They have the best DJs and the slamming-est tunes. You can sit back and relax on a bunch of clouds or fall to your death on some sharp thingies—so STAY AWAY FROM THE EDGE! There's also a photo booth where you can take pictures with your besties (and second besties) as a souvenir from a great night out.

There's no such thing as "second besties."

N.E.WAYZ

THE BOUNCE LOUNGE IS TOTES FER REALZ THE BEST DIMENSION IN ALL THE DIMENSIONS.

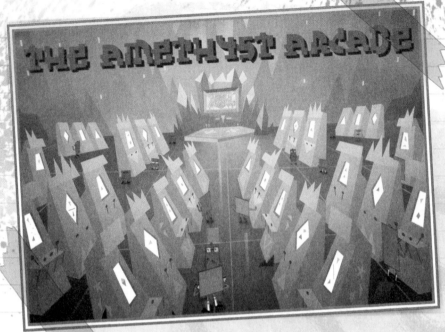

THE AMETHYST ARCADE

The Amethyst Arcade is a rest stop on the way to the Galactic Vortex. It's got every kind of video game, from single-player sleepers like <u>Cloudwatching</u> to high-stakes games like <u>Win or Lose Everything,</u> where you can actually lose everything!

— — — — — — — — — *Including all of your arm hair.*

The arcade is ruled by the Squares, who are all connected to one another and share one mind. Sounds kinda intense, but they are actually pretty chill. I like the Amethyst Arcade because nobody judges you there. You can be yourself.

LIKE, EVEN NERDS ARE TREATED LIKE PEOPLE THERE, RIGHT, MARCO? *What's that supposed to mean?*

It's also a great place to go and challenge your friend to a game of <u>Lance Lance Revolution.</u>

And submit them to a crushing defeat. :)

TRY BEATING ME WHEN I'M NOT BEING CHASED BY

THE FUZZ, E-TURD.

Dimension of Cats with Human Faces

Just look at this picture. . . . I mean . . . enough said.

The Sandwich Dimension

If you're dimension hopping and in need of a bite, don't go to the Sandwich Dimension unless you want to BE the bite. I almost died there. Twice.

If you want to have the most delicious sandwich in the universe, isn't it worth risking your life? The answer is yes! The Sandwich Dimension is a treasure chest of some of the finest sandwiches ever, nestled inside the guts of deadly sandwich monsters.

Do you like pixies? Do you think they are tiny and adorable and sweet? Do you think that having glittery wings makes you good? Well, then, you don't know jack about pixies. Be careful with your interdimensional mirror service when the pixies are your service provider. They don't take Earth money, only gold and jewels. And if you don't have any? They throw you in the Shard Mines to work off your bill—and there's no magic allowed in that gloomy, dark place.

If the Pixie Empress asks you to marry her, SAY NO! Because if you say yes and then change your mind, she gets really REALLY mad and may try to kill you and all your friends. Oh, and she may want to eat you, too. Or maybe she wants to marry you AND eat you?

Earth

Uh . . . that's not Earth. . . . It's my house.

Earth is the third planet from the sun in the Milky Way Galaxy. It's also Marco's home. It's mostly water, so when astronauts take pictures of it from outer space it looks like a big blue-and-green bouncy ball. There isn't really magic on Earth like there is in other dimensions. There are no monsters. . . . But there ARE toilets, which are fun to flush things down. Where the water goes, nobody knows. . . . It's one of Earth's greeeeeeeat-est mysteries.

Whenever Star or her dad, King Butterfly, put stuff in the toilet, it always overflows and my socks get wet. SO. GROSS.

33

The interdimensional clearinghouse for anything and everything magical that you could ever want. Also, they have great sales on things that murder! Quest Buy is so big that you can get lost in there if you're not careful. Actually, getting lost is the only option. If you're found, you're doing it wrong.

I almost died at Quest Buy. Twice. The first time I went to QB, I got electrocuted by a wand charger, and then Ludo's crew almost eviscerated me. The second time, Star got me a murderous gift card, and I was forced by threat of death to buy a security wallet with it. I really liked the wallet until it was stolen by a shifty, joy-sucking birthday magician. I can't believe I just wrote that, or that those things happened to me.

MEWNI

Ahhhh, Mewni! My favorite, and probably the best dimension anywhere.

UH . . . HULLO, BOUNCE LOUNGE?!

Mewni* has everything: waterfalls, caves, mountains, oceans, rivers, clouds, monsters, Mewmans, Pony Heads . . . No indoor plumbing . . . :/

It's also got a lot of boring stuff, too. At least for me. That's why I used to go and pick fights with monsters in the Forest of Certain Death. When Ludo's castle was there, I used to put pig-goat droppings on his doorstep, knock on the door, and run. Hilarious! In addition to Butterfly Castle, where my family lives, there are also other kingdoms in Mewni.

*WANNA SEE A MAP OF MEWNI? TURN TO THE BACK OF THE BOOK. SEE IT? YOU'RE WELCOME!!

35

Our kingdom includes Butterfly Castle and the surrounding lands. It is bordered by the kingdom of the Johansens to the east and the kingdom of the Pigeons to the west.

The Butterfly Groundlands

THE UNDERWORLD

Everything below the sewers of Butterfly Castle is referred to as the Underworld. It's ruled by the Lucitors. They basically take care of lava and lost souls. (I think . . . not totally sure.) The Butterflys and Lucitors have a pretty good relationship, even though the Lucitors have a reputation for being kinda aggro. I guess all that heat and moaning can get to you. My ex-boyfriend Tom is a Lucitor. He's heir to the throne, in fact. One day he'll be king of the Underworld.

The Cloud Kingdom of the Pony Heads

Everything between the tip-top of Butterfly Castle and the very edge of outer space is the Pony Head Kingdom. You might be thinking "Who'd want just the clouds?" but the Pony Heads have made it work for them.

UHHH . . . YEAH, WE DID, AND WE HAVE INDOOR PLUMBING!

For a race of bodiless (don't ask) flying pony heads, the clouds are a perfect place. Sometimes, when King Pony Head and my dad are arguing, it mysteriously rains until my dad finally lets KPH have his way. So, you could say there's a lot of power in the clouds.

37

The Kingdom of the Waterfolk

All the rivers, lakes, seas, and oceans outside of Butterfly Castle are the domain of the Waterfolk. Don't call them "seaple." That's the Old World word for them and is considered offensive. It's said the origins of their kingdom date back to a time when people were so bad at carpentry that their homes kept falling into the seas and rivers. This happened for millennia, and many perished before the people adapted to breathing in the water. They eventually stopped building on land and just stayed underwater. That said, the ~~seaple~~ Waterfolk are known more for their adaptability than their intelligence ... to put it nicely. If you've ever heard the phrase "You're as dumb as a merman," well ... that's where it comes from.

Delphinidae

Like most people from Earth, you probably heart dolphins. When those "save a dolphin" commercials come on TV with a dolphin swimming in human garbage or wearing an old shoe for a hat, a single tear rolls down your cheek. Well, you can stop feeling bad for the dolphins, because they have their own dimension: Delphinidae.

GUESS WHAT? THEY'RE TOTAL JERKS.

The Delphinidaes are rude and bossy. You're just chillin', minding your own business, and then a dolphin gets in your face and yells, "Make me a sandwich!" and you gotta do it. It's illegal to ignore a dolphin in Delphinidae. It happens enough times, and suddenly, dolphins aren't cute anymore. So why go there at all, you ask? No one goes to Delphinidae on purpose. *Don't you mean on porpoise?* :)

Much like a pancake house, you just sorta end up there after a night out when everything else is closed. Roll with it, but beware.

Do you like tea? How about having your brain washed? Neither? Then stay the heck away from St. Olga's Reform School for Wayward Princesses! It looks like a prissy girls' finishing school, but it's really an individuality-destroying police state. . . . "Freethinking" is not the catchword of the day at St. Olga's. Beware the Solitary Conform-ment Chamber, where your free will is overwritten by boring princess etiquette slide shows. If you don't know what a slide show is, it's like if TV was slow and boring.

I almost died at St. O's. Twice. The first time was at the hands of some robot guards, and the second time I almost died emotionally in the Solitary Conform-ment Chamber. I did learn that I'd make a great princess. I really wouldn't say that pink is my color . . . but I wouldn't mind wearing a poofy dress every now and then. It's kinda liberating.

OKAY, SO, YES, ST. O'S USED TO BE A SCARY BRAINWASH DUNGEON, BUT AFTER I LED THE REBELLION, ~~YOU led the rebellion?!~~ THE HEADMISTRESS, MISS HEINOUS, COULDN'T HANG. SO SHE SPLIT, AND ALL THE TEACHERS WERE LIKE, "WE NEED TO GET PAID OR WE CAN'T TEACH," AND I WAS ALL LIKE, "IF YOU NEED TO GET PAID THEN WHY DID YOU BECOME A TEACHER IN THE FIRST PLACE?" BOOM! SO ALL THE TEACHERS LEFT AND THEN ST. O'S BECAME LIKE A TOTAL PARTY SCHOOL! WHICH WAS AWESOME! THEN ALL THE PRINCESSES GOT ALL DEMANDING AND WERE LIKE, "PONY HEAD, WE STILL WANT TO GET AN EDUCATION." AND I WAS ALL LIKE, "EXCUSE ME? DID YOU SAY SOMETHING? I AM SORRY I DID NOT HEAR YOU I WAS ASLEEP CUZ YOU WERE BORING ME TALKING ABOUT EDUCATION." OH! AND THEN THEY KEPT BEING LIKE, "PONY HEAD, WE NEED FOOD. PONY HEAD, THE LIGHTS DON'T WORK. PONY HEAD THIS, PONY HEAD THAT." FINALLY, I WAS JUST LIKE, "OKAY, THIS PLACE IS BORING! PEACE OUT!"

☆ Choose Your Own Dimension ☆

Speaking of dimension hopping . . . this is Roy

Roy travels the dimensions in his Goblin Dog truck, looking for worthy recipients of his otherworldly Goblin Dogs. Think of him as the Santa of processed meat. Everybody loves a Goblin Dog . . . only problem is the Goblin Dog truck is a little tough to find.

PONY HEAD'S ADVICE FOR BRAVING THE LINE AT THE GOBLIN DOG TRUCK

I'VE EATEN A MIL GOBLIN DOGS.   *I think we've established that that is a lie.*

LIKE MORE THAN A MIL. LIKE A ZIL. AND YOU GOTZ TO BE CHILL. CUZ IT'Z A LONG LINE AND YOU WILL WAIT 4EVA. UNLESS YOU ARE A VIP (VERY IMPORTANT PONY) OR YOU GO WITH A VIP. LIKE ME. BUT YOU CAN'T GO WITH ME, CUZ THIS VIP IS TAKEN, RIGHT, B-FLY? SO JUST DON'T GO TO THE GOBLIN TRUCK, CUZ YOU WON'T GET ANY GOBLIN DOGS WITHOUT ME. XOXOXO

Smithsonia

Floats in the air

On this page, feel free to draw the kind of dimension you'd like to visit, and make it super awesome so that Roy will bring his truck there.

• Dimensional Scissors

If you want to travel to other dimensions, you gotta have these!

Dimensional scissors are not easy to get . . . unless you "borrow" them from your parents or steal some like Pony Head did. It's totally up to Hekapoo who receives them. She's a magical being who forges all the dimensional scissors. She's the only being in the multiverse with this ability.

UHHHHHH . . . ACTUALLY, I FOUND THEM IN THE BATHROOM AT THE BOUNCE LOUNGE . . . GYFs.

Using the scissors is complicated, and involves a thorough understanding of the space-time continuum and multiverse theory. . . .

GURL, I JUST USE 'EM LIKE A PAIR OF SCISSORS . . . NO SPACE-TIME CONTINUATION NECESSARY.

Okay. You do kinda just use them like normal scissors. You take the sharp parts and make a little tear in the fabric of space-time. But you gotta really think about where you want to go or you could end up someplace terrible.

Like St. O's, where I almost died. Twice.

Princesses aren't the only ones with dimensional scissors. Some of the bad guys got 'em, too.

Like Ludo. His have a set of horns on them that look like his skull hat.

44

Design and Decorate Your Own Dimensional Scissors

Each pair is special, so make one unique to you!

Cut along dotted line!

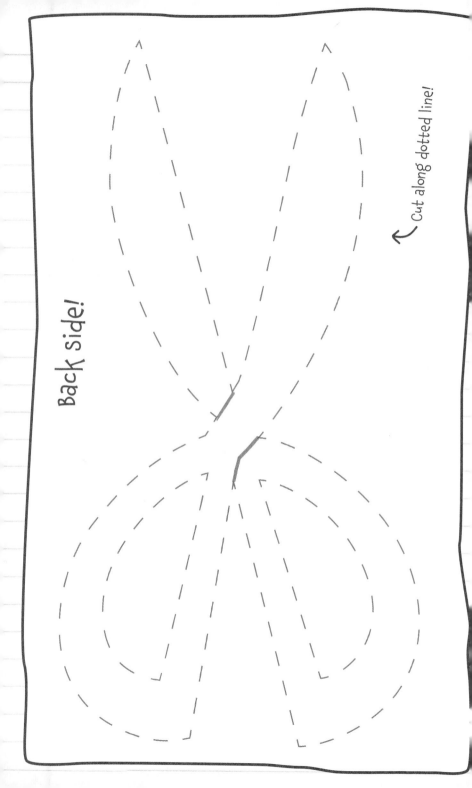

Back side!

Cut along dotted line!

How to Turn Earth into Your Home

Tower Spawn 101 · ◉ · ◉ · ◉ · ◉ ·

Earth is awesome, but if you're a magical princess from another dimension, you'll notice that Earth neighborhoods lack castles. So! I recommend making your Earth home feel more like your <u>home</u> home by turning your room into a princess tower. Here's a step-by-step guide:

1. Go into your Earth room. You will recognize it from the feeling of boredom that it gives you.

2. Think of an un-boring princess tower and point your wand at the ceiling.

3. Yell "Sparkle Glitter Bomb Expand!" and . . .

4. Blast! Watch your princess tower grow in your new home.

Some people might not want their homes remodeled by a visitor from another dimension, but in the case of the Diazes, well . . . I never asked. :)

Whatever you do, DON'T use the Mystic Room-Suck Transform spell, or you'll end up with a black hole that sucks down all the important things you need from your bedroom . . . like your bed and your clothes . . . and, you know, <u>stuff</u>.

47

Top Level

Staircase to Dome:
Wonder what's up there? :)

Werewolf Poster: Rarararararararr!!!

Middle Level

Sea Captain Portrait
I think that guy spoke to me once.

Balcony: I can launch fireworks from
here. Not sayin' I have . . . but I could.

Aquarium: Awwwwww . . .
little puffer!

48

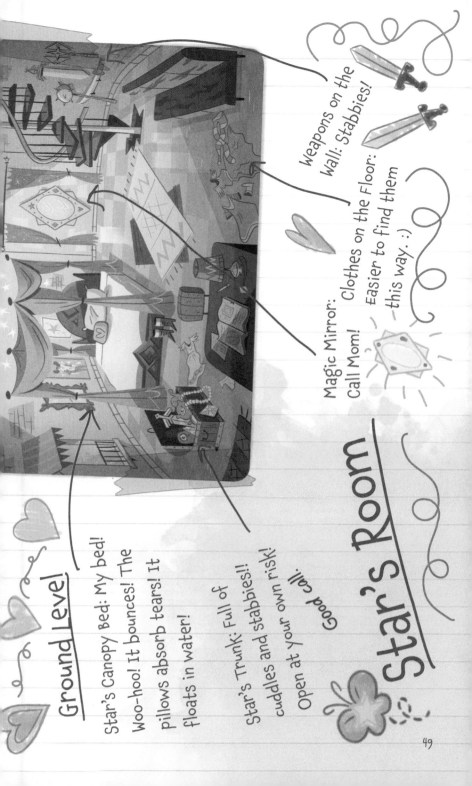

Ground Level

Star's Canopy Bed: My bed! Woo-hoo! It bounces! The pillows absorb tears! It floats in water!

Star's Trunk: Full of cuddles and stabbies!! Open at your own risk!

Good call.

Weapons on the Wall: Stabbies!

Magic Mirror: Call Mom!

Clothes on the Floor: Easier to find them this way. :)

Star's Room

What Goes Down?
Star Explains the Toilet

There is a magical place in the Diaz house that I like to call the bathroom, even though Earth has lots of other names for it . . . like restroom. No one really rests there, but sometimes when I'm in the bathtub I fall asleep.   *But you could drown!*

On it, Marco. I'll just do a spell to make the bubbles in the bubble bath wake me up.   *Oh, okay.*

It can also be called the water closet . . . or powder room . . . or toilet . . . which is confusing, because there is already a toilet in the toilet.
    That's kinda true. I never thought of that before.

The toilet is the center of the bathroom's magic. That's why its nickname is the throne.
                    That's only what my dad calls it.

It's full of crystal-blue water that's so clear you can see your reflection in it. You pull the magic lever on the toilet and the water disappears . . . but then it comes back! And where does it go? No one can be sure, but it's likely that toilet is an entryway to a bunch of tiny waterslides that run through your house.

There are lots of objects you can send down the waterslides, but here are some of my favorites:

—Bowling balls (They are heavy and round and very hard to get into the toilet.)

—Anything alive (Living creatures are afraid of the toilet and will fight you.)

—Laser puppies (See "anything alive" above.)

—Hopes and dreams (Write them on some toilet paper and send them down. You never know who's at the other end to read them, but maybe they'll come true!)

—Marco's hoodie **Nope, we're not going there.**

—Glossaryck (See "anything alive" above.)

—Glitter (Goes down easy and looks like fireworks in the toilet as it spirals down the drain.)

2 COOL 4 SCHOOL

How to Be the Best Exchange Student: Don't Be Gustav (Star Explains)

If there's one thing I learned being an interdimensional exchange student, I'm not sure what it would be. I do know that the Diazes have had a lot of exchange students.

Their first exchange student was Daniella from Belgium. She liked Marco enough to kiss him on the cheek, apparently, but he won't talk about it.

That's right, he won't.

Then there was Pippo the Italian; he never wore a shirt (except for this picture) but he did wear a lot of body spray.

Sometimes when it's quiet at night, I can still smell Pippo.

Next was Akil from Egypt. He played guitar in a speed-metal band. His band was called SlaughterHorse Five but it was just him and a drum machine.

His English wasn't great, but you'd always know if he liked something or not by how many "metals" it was. Like, he LOVED barbecue sauce, so whenever we got chicken wings he'd say "Four metals," holding up his hand with all four fingers out. School was "No metals"; my mom and dad were "Three metals," making them second to barbecue sauce. I never told them, because I didn't want to hurt their feelings.

The year before I arrived, the Diazes hosted Klaus from Switzerland. Klaus was very private.

He put a lock on his door . . . from the inside. I saw him the day he moved in and the day he moved out.

53

Anyway, back to Gustav. As it turns out, Scandinavia is not a physical place on a map. Gustav was really from Bakersfieldville. The Diazes didn't quite put that together before they let him into their hearts. I didn't want to bum them out, and if you're reading this, please don't tell Marco.

Wait . . . what?!

Anyway, if you ever find yourself in the position of being an exchange student, here are some things to avoid:

1. Meat. Don't do anything with meat when you're living at someone else's house. Don't make meatballs. Don't even use the word "meat." It's creepy.

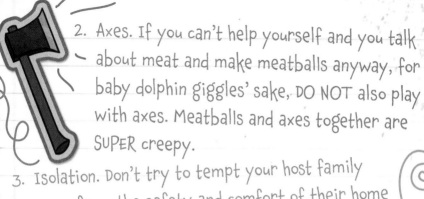

2. Axes. If you can't help yourself and you talk about meat and make meatballs anyway, for baby dolphin giggles' sake, DO NOT also play with axes. Meatballs and axes together are SUPER creepy.

3. Isolation. Don't try to tempt your host family away from the safety and comfort of their home by offering to take them out into an isolated part of the woods, ESPECIALLY if you already made meatballs and played with axes. These three things together create a creep-trinity.

Try these instead:

1. Water. Nothing says "thank you" like filling your host family's house with thousands of gallons of water and turning it into a water park.

2. Hair. Alternately, you can fill your host family's house with a giant beard.

3. Puppies. This is a no-brainer, because even the most anti-pet member of the household can't resist a litter of puppies. If they have dangerous laser eyes, try to remind your host family how cute they are.

Star, this is going to be your new school.

Echo Creek Academy

PLEASE READ.
LOVE,
DADDY

"Is this the moon? No, it's Echo Creek."

You'd never know it by looking at this gem of a town today, but before the settlers arrived, the city of Echo Creek, in the heart of the cement-lined Echo Creek River Valley, was once regarded as "Nature's Landfill"—a place where Mother Nature put all of her garbage.

But a group of settlers saw something very different when they arrived here 104 years ago. After a harrowing winter trek through the Mt. St. Angelus Mountains, the Bonner Party, a group of

Echo Creek Academy

seventeen pilgrims, decided to settle and incorporate the city of Echo Creek in 1898. Though it wasn't the place they were seeking, Bonson Bonner, the group's leader, assured his clan that they were en route to the moon. They nonetheless found the charm of Nature's Landfill adequate.

Little did they know the land they settled was already occupied. After the historic Twenty-Six-Day War, the Bonners were able to fight off a savage band of opossums and claim the land for people. The Bonners valued nothing more than education, and as the last opossum, Otis, was sent scurrying to the surrounding forest, Echo Creek Academy was built on this very spot.

The original school was constructed of "whitewood"; today we know it as mammoth bone. As it turns out, Echo Creek sits atop a mud pit that may have ensnared mammoths on their way to find warmth during the Great Enfreezening (we're not really sure). To this day, the entire basement of Echo Creek Academy is still made of mammoth bones.

And what a foundation for such a place of learning! You can get a sense of the history of Echo Creek just walking the halls of Echo Creek Academy. Our principal, Edwin Bonner-Skeeves, a descendent of Bonson Bonner, carries the mission of the Bonner Party into his management of the school.

"It may not be the moon, but the city of Echo Creek has a lot to offer: we have our own stolen water, a racetrack, a great Jet Ski dealership, and, as far as learning is concerned, Echo Creek Academy is a completely adequate place to spend a lot of money on an education. As principal of Echo Creek Academy, I say no one values your child's education more than you. I encourage parents to have nightly check-ins with their children. Ask the tough questions: Did your teacher show up today? Was your teacher awake? Fix your kids' homework for them so they can slip through the cracks in the education system. It's like I always say: failure is just mediocrity that fell down the stairs. As a parent, it's your job to be at the top of the stairs, looking mediocrity in the eye and say 'Don't fall.' Are we done with the interview?"

Principal Bonner-Skeeves

Echo Creek Academy Freshman Class
2014-2015

ECHO CREEK ACADEMY

Star Butterfly
Marco Diaz
Jackie-Lynn Thomas
Janna Ordonia

You're the best . . . so much fun having you in Echo Creek!

see you this summer! Jackie-Lynn

See you in Marco's clo... after he's aslee... Janna

Ferguson O'durguson
Alfonzo Dolittle
Francis Smithington
Lars Vanderdud
Justin Armberg

Can you turn us back into a centaur? Ferguson & Alfonzo

Later Nurd! LARS

Star Butterfly RULEZ! Justin

Brittney Wong
Sabrina Backintosh
Hope Hadley
Moobs Squitson

I wish this pen wrote with fire Brittney

It was worth the hospital visit! Sabrina

-Thanks for the magic! Hope

Thanks for the pie. moobs

Starfan13
Raya Rousey
Blake Lemons
Megan Gandlym

Ever get that feeling like someone's watching you? It's prolly me! I LOVE YOU SO MUCH! SINCERELY, STARFAN13

Call me this summer. or not. -Raya

I'm never borrowing your scissors again! Blake

Thanks for ruining the football field so I didn't have to cheerlead anymore. -Megan

Ingrid Bloomgren
Chelsea McNelsey

DAS SIEHT AUS WIE Tinte, ist es ABER NICHT, HAB EINEN schoenen Sommer! INGRID

Look out for the Fall Hall! Chelsea

27

OSKAR-KHESTRA
LANCE OF ENTRANCE-MENT
ALBUM DROP

BOOM! The BIGGEST ALBUM OF THE CENTURY has hit this decade. <u>Lance of Entrance-ment</u> (the seventh not-full-studio album release by Oskar-Khestra [aka, the artist formerly now known as Oskar Greason]) has been dropped.

About This Bombastic Music:

<u>Lance of Entrance-ment</u> is like nothing you've ever heard: thirteen solid minutes of dub-house trance thrash featuring the mind-bending keytar psychedelia of Oskar Greason (aka, the artist who is also known as Oskar-Khestra).

This one music blog says: "Oskar Greason is so good at what he does and yet so humble. Stop and think about that. Why don't you let go and let Oskar take you into the depths of his musical mind-tunnel with these five tracks? I can't believe he's just giving this music away. . . . It's like he's like one of those people who helps starving children, only he does that for our ears . . . with music. Like if your ears were hungry, then what would be the food? Music, right?"

Track listing:

1. Mom, Don't Tell Me What to Do!

2. Twinkle, Twinkle

3. I Don't Like Your Boyfriend, Mom!

4. Little Book Dude
   (feat. Glossaryck)

5. Wish Upon a Car
   (instrumental)

HEAR OSKAR'S TUNES AND DOWNLOAD HIS LATEST INSTRUMENTAL TO WRITE YOUR OWN LYRICS. TWITTER.COM/OSKARKHESTRA

St. Olga's

The One True Path to Reformation: Transcending Your Personality and Becoming a Proper Princess

by Miss Heinous

Don't allow your noble lineage to be thrown away. Trust in St. Olga's to have a plethora of foolproof measures to turn your troublemaking princess into a paragon of proper society.

Here at St Olga's, we employ all the tricks of the trade:

- The all-seeing Clock of Cinnadale
- Purity isolation chambers for hard cases
- No mail in or out
- Premises encircled by the Bottomless Moat of Oblivion
- Anti-dimensional scissor Tramolfidian Crystal Tower
- Dragon-proof shingles
- Unbreakable stained glass
- Escape-proof room-cells

IT'S NOT CRIMINAL TO BE AN INDIVIDUAL

IT'S NOT CRIMINAL TO BE

IT'S NOT CRIMINAL TO BE AN INDIVIDUAL

If your elbows are on the Table you belong in a Stable

Etiquette is the main focus for your troubled wayward princess. We turn undisciplined behavior into perfection.

We at St. Olga's believe a princess should be seen and not heard. We teach all our students to:

- Dress appropriately
- Practice proper throne posture
- Remain silent
- Keep their pinkies at a ninety-degree angle when drinking tea

And not to:

- Talk with their mouths full
- Have any opinions at all

Your freethinking one-in-a-million brat will become a one-of-a-million emotionless rubber stamp your bloodline can count on.

At St Olga's, we will break them of all their bad habits.

- Too wild?
- Too opinionated?
- Too bubbly?
- Too sassy?

Too bad! After a stint at St. Olga's, you can kiss all that nasty individuality good-bye!

A princess who Misbehaves will be saved in the Solitary Conform-ment Chamber

IT'S NOT CRIMINAL TO BE AN INDIVIDUAL

INDIVIDUAL

CLIQUES, CREWS, MONSTERS

Wanted: the Forces of Evil

HEY, B-FLY! I FOUND THESE FLYERS WHEN I WAS AT THE INTERDIMENSIONAL POLICE STATION. . . . OMG, DID U KNOW THAT TOFFEE GUY YOU TOLD ME ABOUT IS MOST WANTED? THAT'S HOT!

What were you doing at the police station?

MYOB EARTHTURD

I'm not sure that's the same guy. . . .

It's <u>TOTALLY</u> the same guy.

But I thought he blew up?

Guess not?

W/E HE'S HOT!

WANTED

MOST WANTED IN ALL DIMENSIONS BY ORDER OF THE MAGIC HIGH COMMISSION

MIA

Toffee
aka Toffee of Septarsis

Wanted for the attempted theft of magical items (magic wand), unlawful imprisonment of magical persons, mass-magical detonation of a royal protected structure and its inhabitants (Castle Avarius), and failure to comply with Mewman/Monster Accord.

Toffee of Septarsis was last seen before the destruction of Castle Avarius. He had taken the castle over, in violation of the Avarius-Septarsis Treaty. He hasn't been seen since the blast that destroyed Castle Avarius but is Septarian and thus capable of regenerating. His ability to fully regenerate is unclear as he was incapable of regenerating after the conflict prior to the Mewman/Monster Accord, wherein he lost a finger that never restored. No part of him has been recovered.

Castle wuh?

You ever heard of this, Star?

WANTED

WANTED IN ALL LANDS BY ORDER OF THE MAGIC HIGH COMMISSION

MIA

OH, LOOK! IT'S LUDO! HE'S A PRINCE? YOU GOT TO BE KIDDING ME!

Ludo
aka Ludo of Mewni,
Prince Ludo of Castle Avarius

Wanted for the attempted theft of magical items (magic wand), mass-magical detonation of a royal protected structure and its inhabitants (Castle Avarius), and failure to comply with Mewman/Monster Accord.

Ludo of Mewni has been missing since the destruction of his home, Castle Avarius, in the protected Groundlands of the kingdom of Queen Butterfly (aka Moon the Undaunted).

WANTED

WANTED IN ALL LANDS BY ORDER OF THE MAGIC HIGH COMMISSION

MIA

Miss Heinous
aka Lady of Conform-ment,
Warden Heinous, Lady of St. Olga's

Most wanted for her crimes against individuality, unlawful conjuring and employment of rogue monsters, and unlawful imprisonment of magic users.

Miss Heinous has been missing since the fall of St. Olga's Reform School for Wayward Princesses. Her whereabouts are unknown. Identifying marks include her cheek emblems (clovers).

SEE? I TOLD YOU THAT WAS WEIRD.

She has secured the services of rogue monster Rasticore Chaosus Disastervaine, a known bounty hunter and violator of the Mewman/Monster Accord.

65

WANTED

OH, HE'S HOT, TOO!

EWWWW... Pony!

Rasticore
aka Rasticore Chaosus Disastervaine, RCD, Rasticore the Bounty Hunter, Rasticore of Septarsis

Most wanted for crimes of unlawful pursuit of magic persons, unlawful alteration of unregistered, protected magic items (dimensional scissors), and destruction of magical property in a protected area (Quest Buy).

Rasticore Chaosus Disastervaine was last seen in Quest Buy. Initially, he was thought to be destroyed after a misdirected laser attack, but his left hand was not recovered in the aftermath. He's Septarian and can regenerate, possibly from his severed hand.

Good or Force of Evil? You Decide!

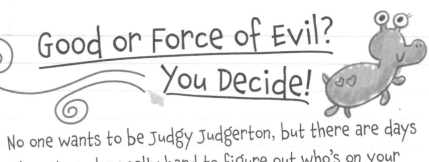

No one wants to be Judgy Judgerton, but there are days when it can be really hard to figure out who's on your team, who's not, and who's . . . uh . . . well, something else. Father Time, King Butterfly, Marco—all good guys, no question. Ludo, Toffee, Miss Heinous—they're all bad news, totes obvi. But we've encountered some weirdy-weirds that we just can't agree on. Take a look and see if you can decide whether or not the folks on this list are good or forces of evil.

WHAT IS THIS?!?

Ewwww . . . Marco . . . did the laser puppies get ahold of this?

That doesn't look like their kind of . . . mess.

? The Truth or Punishment Box

Along with her dimensional scissors, the Truth or Punishment Box is another thing that Pony Head "found" in the bathroom of the Bounce Lounge. That alone would probably be reason enough not to play with it, but I mean, come on. Of course we played with it. But it was such a grump! It kept getting mad and finally self-destructed when it couldn't comprehend our young minds.

? I say the Truth or Punishment Box is good because without the box forcing me to reveal my crush on Jackie-Lynn Thomas I would never have gone to the dance with her or ridden on a skateboard with her.

I say the box is evil because it doesn't understand teenagers!

What do you think?

☐ GOOD ☐ FORCE OF EVIL ☒ UNDECIDED

Buff Frog (aka Yvgeny Bulgolyubov)

I like Buff Frog. He's the cutest gross frog monster I know. It's hard to explain, but my gut says he's good. He ended up turning on Ludo, and he became an awesome dad to a bunch of really sweet li'l tadpole babies.

~BOOP!~

I'm on the fence. He spied on us for Ludo. For about six months I'd look out the window and see him in the tree with binoculars. Creepy. Then there're those babies. . . . I know they're cute, but when I stared deep into their egg whites, it was almost like they were laughing at me in there. Like, what's so funny, tadpoles? Seriously . . . you're tadpoles.
STOP MAKING FUN OF ME.

Okay, Marco . . . you've lost it. Let's let someone else decide.

What do you think?

☐ GOOD   ☐ FORCE OF EVIL   ▨ UNDECIDED

Friends Till the End Gift Card

Now you're REALLY scraping here. That card wasn't even a thing.

She was, too! She worked hard to make sure you found something that you really wanted. And it worked! You love your wallet.

You're just saying that because YOU bought me the card . . . definitely sweet of you . . . BUT YOU DIDN'T READ THE FINE PRINT AND IT ALMOST KILLED US!

So you don't like the wallet?

No, I love the wallet.

So she's good.

The security on the wallet doesn't work and Janna stole my Eggzfan punch card. . . . I had one more punch left to get a free dozen. Sounds evil to me.

Obviously we're not on the same page with this one.

What do you think?

☐ GOOD   📖 FORCE OF EVIL   ☐ UNDECIDED

The Laser Puppies

How'd the laser puppies end up on this list?

> I was *about* to ask you the same thing.

>> Well, let's just check "good." Everyone loves the laser puppies.

Yeah, must be some kind of mistake.

NO, I PUT THEM ON THE LIST. HUH? Pony Head?!

CORRECT. I DO NOT LIKE DOGS, K? GTG.

They aren't dogs, they're laser puppies!

W/E GTG NO DOGZ PLZ.

No, wait! Just look at this:

K, THAT IS PRETTY ADORBS. . . .

See? Told ya!

FINE!

JUST CHECK "GOOD." MOVING ON GTG OMG!

What do you think?

☐ GOOD   ☐ FORCE OF EVIL   UNDECIDED

71

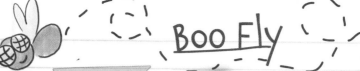

Boo Fly

Boo Fly is a weird little guy. He kidnapped Marco, but he also makes airplane noises with his mouth when he flies, sorta like a five-year-old. It's kinda adorable.

Evil. He worked for Ludo and he kidnapped me. No-brainer.

When he flies, it looks like he's gonna crash into things . . . so cute.

Forget it!

HE KIDNAPPED ME.

What do you think?

☐ GOOD ◼ FORCE OF EVIL ☐ UNDECIDED

Willoughby & Lydia

There's a fence and I am sitting on it. Willoughby is a dog. But in her dimension, dogs aren't like dogs on Earth. They have very complicated feelings. So she stole my wand to make herself not have those complicated feelings anymore.

That's what she says. But she spent a lot of time in the bathroom.

That's where she was trying to make the wand work. In the bathroom mirror. *Yeah . . . hmmm, but what about Lydia?*

Lydia might have been a little dishonest about Willoughby being her dog, but I think it came from a good place.

She made a fake flyer looking for a fake dog.

Because she was lonely. So was Willoughby. Which is why they make such a good team now that they're together for real.

A girl and her wand-stealing dog that spends more time in the bathroom than I do.

I wouldn't necessarily say that. . . .

What do you think?

☐ GOOD   ◼ FORCE OF EVIL   ☐ UNDECIDED

Mina Loveberry

Mina was once Mewni's greatest defender. She even fought alongside my mom on the battlefield! My mom said that even without casting magic spells, Mina was as strong as any monster.

But she's B–A–N–A–N–A–S.

Being an amazing superhero comes at a price. She was pretty messed up, I guess.

She was covered in mud.

Not messed up like <u>messy</u>. Messed up as in <u>messed up</u>. But some of the stuff she taught me <u>was</u> pretty cool. Like how to make my own weapons.

You're already a weapon. You don't need to make any more.

Awwww . . . Thank you, Marco!

What do you think?

☐ GOOD   ☐ FORCE OF EVIL   <u>UNDECIDED</u>

Karate vs. Monsters:
Marco Explains Fighting Techniques

I don't have a wand like Star, but I think what I _do_ have is equal to . . . might I say, maybe even better, than . . . a wand. Because wands have a funny way of backfiring on you and blowing up your house or turning your teacher into a troll or making you grow a beard that takes over the world or trying to kill you.

Karate would never do any of those things. It's too zen. Wands are kind of all about chaos, but karate is totally about finding your center and only attacking from a place of serenity. I've been a student of karate for many years now, and I think I have learned much about the art through my sensei. I have many techniques I can access when subduing monsters.

These are special moves and require knowledge of secret pressure points.

Wow, Marco, I had no idea you were actually doing moves all this time. . . . I thought you were just sorta jammin' out.

The Moves

The Blushing VHS Karate Student move:

From <u>Kiba Dachi</u> (Horse Stance) rotate your right arm so the palm is up. Make a fist. Extend your index finger so it points at your opponent. Crinkle index finger in a "come here" gesture. The monster will laugh at you. Feel brief embarrassment at having done verbatim something you saw in a Mackie Hand movie, then quickly jab the monster in the solar plexus with your right heel. Use your own shame to overcome your opponent.

The Chimichanga <u>Shuto Uchi</u> move:

While eating a chimichanga (I like mine warm, not hot), lift your left hand and karate-chop attacking monster on the side of the neck.

The Stop Talking and Fight move:

Say the monster is talking and you just wanna fight. From <u>Zenkutsu Dachi</u> (Forward-Leaning Stance) yell at the monster. Anything works, really. (Essentially, you are now the one talking, but because you're yelling, the monster will stop talking. Like most martial arts, karate has a sort of system of opposites going for it, where you end up doing things that seem contrary to what you want.) Here is the perfect place to employ a <u>Mae Tobi Geri</u> (Front Flying Kick) to the Vactoid*, using your big toe to activate the pressure point and disable the monster.

I hope all this is helpful to you the next time you find yourself in the middle of a monster attack.

Arigatō,
Marco Diaz

MONSTER PRESSURE POINTS

1. The Herculeanium
Press twice with right index
finger to disable.

2. *The Vactoid
Must be activated with
your big toe.

3. The Boomis
Only works on the second Tuesday
of every other month.
Activate with karate chop.

4. The Nailbow
Vestigial

5. The Writusyck
Punch once to render
monster unconscious.

6. The Bloop
Pinch between thumb and index finger.

7. The Homer
Works sometimes.
Activate with karate chop.

8. The Knucklebuckle
Activate with left-foot kick only.

9. The Asthix
Activate with right-foot kick only.

10. The Corkscrew
Activate with left ring finger.

11. The Needle-Noser
Activate with karate chop.

12. The Hickticker
Vestigial

13. The Vashtipickleelysiumhondocrutchdonut
(more commonly known as: the Ick)
Only use this pressure point as a last resort;
whole monster will explode.

14. The Quix
Press four times to activate.

15. The Razority
Vestigial

BEING PROUD OF WHERE YOU CAME FROM

Mewnipendence Day—
The Thirty-Seventh of Gravnogk

Marco had some issues with the national history of Mewni. Mostly he thought the thirty-seventh of Gravnogk (or Mewnipendence Day, as we call it) seemed like it was . . . uh . . . a little complicated.

Overly violent, maybe?

I had never really thought of it until he pointed it out, but I guess he was right.

You guess?

Maybe it was a little unfair that the Mewmans had magic against the monsters. I'm still convinced the monsters were mostly jerks, though . . . and come on, look how <u>cute</u> this book is.

You cut the book up into pieces?!?
Isn't it from your childhood?

Yes. Because I needed to put it in this book. It's called scrapbooking.

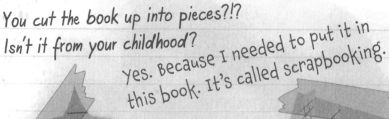

A long time ago, the first settlers of Mewni arrived. A modest people with noble pursuits: life, liberty, and corn.

But the wicked monsters rose up and attacked the innocent Mewmans to take back Mewni for themselves!

So the queen used her magic to turn the simple peasants into a fearsome army.

And then there was fightingfightingfighting
and the Mewmans won!

↰ This part suspiciously lacking detail . . .

Okay . . . it's a little unfair.

Mostly. Mostly.

The Queen Is King, or Matrilineality: The Fact in the Fiction

In Mewni the queen is way more in charge of things than the king is. But even though my mom may call the shots, she also has to do all the super boring royal stuff that my dad doesn't have to do—like running all of Mewni and making all the important decisions for the safety of its people. This happens when you become a queen, because the throne is like a gift—one that gets handed down from queen to queen . . . for, well, ever.

So when the old queen gets tired of being queen and maybe wants to take a vacation, she gives the throne to her daughter? Uh, that doesn't sound like a gift. That sounds like a lot of work and responsibility.

I said it was __like__ a gift, Marco. I didn't say it __was__ one.

Anyway, I think that's why we've only had a few monster uprisings instead of one, like, every day . . . because most of the queens have been pretty good at their job (like my mom). In honor of the awesomeness of queenly stuff, I made this nifty flow chart of what I would do if I were queen tomorrow:

First Order of Business

Send Glossaryck to check on any monster uprisings.

Glossaryck gets captured by monsters.

Appoint Princess Pony Head as Super Secret Oskar Spy.

Forget you sent Glossaryck to check on any monster uprisings.

Turn throne room into Mermaid Grotto.

Ixnay that idea.

Go hang out at the Bounce Lounge with Pony Head.

Get attacked by angry mermaids.

Instead appoint Marco as Super Secret Oskar Spy.

Have an awesome time dancing until you drop.

Ransom newly appointed Super Secret Oskar Spy to get mermaids to stop attacking.

Making queenly decisions isn't that difficult if you don't forget to have fun!

My Dearest Star,

There comes a time in every mother's life when she has to let her child go. It's a very difficult thing, because you know that the world is full of monsters who would seek to harm the child you hold so dear. Yet it is a double-edged sword . . . because the only way for you to acquire the leadership skills you need to someday govern our lands is to go out into the worlds and experience life.

I am cheered by the fact that you have so many tried and true friends, like Marco and Princess Pony Head. I know that they love you, and that on the many adventures you go on together, they will look after you and you will look after them. As you already know, having a strong circle of friendship is the greatest magic of all.

But friendship alone will not always be able to protect you. For those times, you must use real magic. As powerful as your wand is, it is merely a tool to help you access what is already inside of you. I know that Glossaryck "charmingly" refers to it as "dipping down," but I like to think of it as "finding the rainbow inside."

You, my lovely Star, possess the most glorious rainbow of all.

With love,

Mom

My mom is not a big hugger (like my dad is), but sometimes she writes me letters that let me know how much she really loves me.

The Grandma Room

So there's a sorta off-limits room in Butterfly Castle that I'm not REALLY supposed to go in, but I totally went in there when I was a little kid. Aaaaaand maybe I sorta went in there ... traveled inside my wand ... recently ... sorta. Anyway, when I was a kid, the Grandma Room (that's not the official name. ... I think my mom calls it the Tapestry Room) was a smelly old room with wall rugs in it, and each wall rug has one of my grandmas on it. It's still a smelly old room with wall rugs, but my grandmas were all supercool.

Celena the Shy

I knew her as Great-Great-Grandma Shy, and she was BEE-YOO-TIFUL according to everyone. I was like "So what," but my mom explained that her beauty was one of her powers and she was actually able to disarm monsters with a single glance in their direction. Skillz . . . .

What lies behind the golden fan
her hand does sweetly hold?
A trove of cosmic secrets
that never will be told.

Solaria the Monster Carver

A castle stormed is a hero born
with might as strong as steel.
Kneel the void before her
and the crushing force she wields.

Grandma Solaria? Never heard of her. I have a grandma who had a shaved head and carved monsters? HULLO? The only grandma my mom talked about besides Celena was Soupina the Strange. She could use her magic to make . . . uhh . . . soup.

Eclipsa, Queen of Darkness

Before Glossaryck told me she had a locked chapter in my spell book, I had never heard of Eclipsa either. When I found her tapestry, it brought up a lot of questions. . . . I wonder why my mom never mentioned her. I mean, I read her chapter. It was dark, but sorta meh. What's the big deal?

Eclipsa, Queen of Mewni,
to a Mewman king was wed,
but took a monster for her love
and away from Mewni fled.

Festivia the Fun

When the threat of monsters at the gate
has darkened out the sun,
let the kingdom find some peace and joy
in Festivia the Fun.

Mewni's original party girl. She kept the people happy when war was waging outside the gates, and I hear she also had a pretty wicked wand blast.

Skywynne, Queen of Hours

Skywynne is one of my most respected grannies. She added a lot of great spells to the book; most of them involve time and movement.

Ticktock the clock talks,
but secret are its powers.
The only one to break its spell
is Skywynne, Queen of Hours.

Moon the Undaunted

Not a grandma yet. ;)

The immortal monster
will long be haunted
by the darkest spell of
Moon the Undaunted.

My mom? Little Chauncey? My mom being a rad spell-blasting lady with hot go-go power boots?! Toffee?! Glossaryck?! Toffee's losing a finger to . . . my mom?! ugh . . . so many questions . . .

STAR AND GLOSSARYCK'S
GUIDE TO MAGIC

Share Your Magic with the World

Marco's always asking me how my wand
works, how spells work, etc.

I am?

Yeah, dude, that one time you did.

*Yeah, once. But you said "always." I asked
once and I was confused.*

Little over your head?

Yeah . . . a little over yours, too.

So here's an FAQ of frequently asked questions.

Star, FAQ stands for "frequently asked questions."

Q: Where do your spells come from?
A: Not sure. Next question.

Q: How come sometimes you call a spell out, and
sometimes you just blast without naming the spell?

A: Sheesh, now you're getting all technical.

Star, who are you talking to?

A wand blast is different from a spell. A spell is specific, but a wand blast is just a wild-card shot. It's like when you're in a restaurant and you order food. Sometimes you say "I'd like a cheese sandwich on farmer's rye with lettuce, tomatoes, grainy mustard, and sweet pickles." Other times you just go "Gimme the chef's special." That's a wand blast—the chef's special. You never know what's gonna come out.

Q: Do you write your spells down?
  A: Not really.

Q: Really? But aren't you worried you'll forget them?
  A: Nah . . . not really . . . my mind's a steel trap.

Q: So you remember all of them?
  A: Mmmmmaybe?

Q: Hey, I thought I was the one asking the questions!
  A: I don't even know who you are!
        Yeah, who is this person?
It's just an FAQ, Marco, it's not a real person . . . duh.
        Then why are you arguing with them?

Q: I don't wanna argue. . . .
  A: Good! Me neither!

Q: So . . . you <u>do</u> remember all your spells?
  A: Hmmmmm . . . lemme see . . .

Star Butterfly's Magical Compendium of Superfantastic Self-Starting Spells!*

(*Wand not included)

Okay, I don't remember all my spells, but I remember the ones I use a lot. When calling a spell out, I sorta try to cast what I think I need in that moment, but sometimes I just end up going with whatever is on the tip of my tongue.

My spells usually involve animals, bugs, food, rainbows, forces of nature, and sometimes a combo of all the above. Here are some of my favorites.

Time Spells

Glitter Grenade Rewind

Can't find the remote? Use this to rewind your favorite program/ruin your television! Remember, clockworks tick a lot, so this spell can make your television tick like a clock.

I'll just use the remote, thanks.

Easy Peasy Time Freezy

Uh . . . just don't. But if you must, try Easy Peasy Time Un-Freezy to undo it.

Star couldn't get the Un-Freezy one to work. We had to go to the Plains of Time and do a bunch of stuff to fix it. But it pretty much worked out in the end.

Animal Family Spells

These spells have animal magic in them. Animal magic is the sweetest magic that exists, and it leaves behind a mild scent of singed marshmallow after you've used it. Yum!

Bunny Rocket Blast (aka Rabbit Rocket Blast)

This spell uses bunny-powered throttle to propel you forward. It's a pretty easy spell to master, and you can use it a lot when you don't wanna walk using your feet.

You can't always use magic to get where you want to go, Star. And walking is heart-healthy.

Narwhal Blast (aka Nightmare Narwhal Blast and Mega Narwhal Blast)

A stalwart in the ol' spell arsenal. Perhaps my favorite and most effective blasting spell. Because nothing else pummels like a narwhal. And they're supercute, to boot.

Narwhals also have very pointy horns that can catch on the sleeve of your hoodie and rip it.

That never happened, Marco.

But it could.

Warnicorn Stampede

Warnicorn Stampede is one of the spell-iest spells from the family spell book. This spell unleashes a stampede of muscly warnicorns upon whoever is in front of my wand when I cast it. I'm not sure which of my great-grannies invented this spell, but whoever she was, she was hardcore.

Force of Nature Spells

These spells have natural magic inside them. I am not a fan of some natural magic spells because they can make me sneeze a bunch of times in a row. *Maybe you're allergic to those spells?*

Hmmm . . . veeery interesting thought, Marco. I shall have to research this idea of yours.

Stardust Daisy Devastation

A little bit of the power of the sun with a little bit of daisies! It creates a bunch of flower petal explosions and one big daisy firework display at the end. Makes a great Mother's Day gift if you don't like your mother. This spell does <u>not</u> make me sneez

Winterstorm Hyperblow

Perfect for freezing angry pixies when they maybe want to kill you and your friends. It relies on the power of snowflakes . . . which seem cute and adorable, but really they're more like scary baby ice monsters with sharp icicle teeth. This spell also does not make me sneeze.

General Attack Spells

These spells have both defensive and offensive uses. And I like to think that a good offense can be worth a bird in the hand.
I don't even think that's a metaphor anymore.

Mega-Explosive Crystal Laser

Supposedly this is one of the most destructive spells in the book, capable of neutralizing entire planets, but I just use it to distract large cats.

Insect Family Spells

These spells have insect magic inside them. **What's insect** It's the kind of magic that comes from insects, **magic?** Marco. Which means you have to be very nice to all the insects you meet. Otherwise, they get offended.

How can you even know when an insect is offended? They're so small. Trust me, you know.

Turbo Nuclear Butterfly Blast

For when you absolutely gotta wipe out every monster in the yard (with rainbows and butterflies).

This is a great spell. Although, it once gave me a headache from being in the blast radius.

Supersonic Leech Bomb

Send a flurry of adorable radioactive leeches at your enemy. The leeches are super nice about the whole thing. They like meeting new people, so it's kinda like you're doing them a favor.

Dagger Heart Blast (aka Dagger Crystal Heart Attack)

Imagine a million little paper cuts, each infecting the target with a bit of heartache. Now don't imagine anymore. Because that's what it does.

That sounds painful.

You have no idea, Marco.

Rainbow Family Spells

These spells are all rainbow-driven. From tiny prism-size rainbows to giant double rainbows, rainbow spells have a lot of power behind them.

Rainbow Fist Punch

Rainbow Fist Punch is great for leveling the playing field with BIG monsters. Sometimes I sorta use it unfairly against little monsters, too, but only if they're really annoying.

Super Rainbow Dolphin Slap

I just like the sound of it. I don't use it very often. I don't like to, uh, bother the dolphin. It feels kinda rude to ask him to stop everything he's doing and go slap monsters around for you.

Transformation Spells

These spells make things into other things.

Mystic Room-Suck Transform

Turn any room into a disappeared version of itself! Where does it go? Nobody knows!

I hate this spell. My room has never been the same. Not since Star used this spell on it.

Spells You Can Eat

No, don't eat these . . . seriously.

She means it. From experience, I can say she is *100* percent correct.

Poison Crystal Cupcake Kiss (aka Cupcake Blast)

Tastes like a cupcake but poisons like a witch's kiss.

This may look, smell, and taste like a chocolate, vanilla, butterscotch, or strawberry cupcake, BUT IT IS NOT. It will do damage to your intestines and make you not a happy camper for many, many hours.

Syrup Tsunami Shock Wave

This spell has syrup and waffles in it. I don't know how they get them in there. It's kinda spooky. But it makes everything it touches as sticky as molasses.

Once again, this spell may look, smell, and taste like waffles with syrup on them—BUT IT IS NOT. Just remember these words: not a happy camper.

Returneo Armeo Normalredicus
(aka Armeo and Armeus Normalreno)

Supposed to cure Releaseo Demonius Infestica (better known as Monster Arm). This was a spell I once did on Marco and it caused a lot of, uh, <u>problems</u>. So . . . hope the cure worked!

I think so. I <u>hope</u> so. Is there a chance it didn't work?

Oh, I'm sure it's fine, Marco. Your arm looks pretty normal these days.

Spells I'm Never Supposed to Talk About

Shhh . . . we're not supposed to talk about these spells.

~~The All-Seeing Eye~~

~~Look, I can't talk~~

~~about this.~~

~~The Whispering Spell~~

~~Seriously . . .~~

~~I can't.~~

Greetings from Inside Your Book of Spells

Hello,

Princess Butterfly!

Welcome to your new Magic Instruction Book!
I'm Sir Glossaryck of Terms, at your service,
m'lady. I'm here to help you reach your potential.
I live inside your book, so always knock before
opening and <u>never</u> put peanut butter between the
pages—no, wait, that's not what I meant to say. . . .
What I meant to say is <u>always</u> put peanut butter
between the pages. Peanut butter will be eaten,
but try to think of this book like a library book—
something that's yours for now but later will be
someone else's. And like a library book, you
might not finish reading it before you have to
give it back.

You'll notice throughout your Magic
Instruction Book many different languages,
drawings, maps, and other scrawlings that,
when you squint, look important (see fig.1a).

Well, they are important! But they won't all
make sense to you when you first encounter
them. This means you aren't ready for them,
so move forward to
something that you
do understand.

fig.1b

Does the above diagram
(fig.1b) make sense?

It does? Fantastic! Let's start there, with
Make Me a Burger! Perfect, you're already
understanding how your book works. Also, thank
you for the burger! (If you're reading this and
still have not made me a burger then make me
a burger. Seriously. Do it now. I'll wait.)

Me, You, Magic, Your Magic Instruction Book, Etc.

Okay, so now you're probably itching to get going with your Magic Instruction Book and start learning magic so you can do "sweet moves" and zonk some baddies or something. . . . Well, this is where I tell you the MOST IMPORTANT THING YOU OUGHT TO KNOW ABOUT ME, YOU, MAGIC, YOUR MAGIC INSTRUCTION BOOK, ETC.—the thing you're going to ignore forever, but you absolutely oughtn't to (but you will, so you may as well skip ahead to the next part).

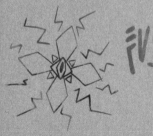

I Knew You Would Skip Ahead

So, you skipped ahead, just like I figured. Didn't even read a word of my very

important message for you. Now we are in the best place to begin.

fig.1c

So this is you (fig.1c). You've opened your book,

found this page, and you're looking at a picture of yourself looking at this page. If this is what you're seeing, then your Magic Instruction Book should be calibrated correctly. If you're seeing this:

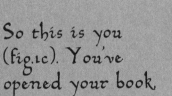

fig.1d

then bring me a burger already! Also, if you're seeing this, your spell book will

not be properly calibrated. Go back and try again, but bring me the burger, too.

Why Me?

"Ugh!" the princess hollered as she threw her wand down on the floor. "Why do I have to listen to this STUPID Glossaryck?!"

Sound familiar? Well, you're gonna say it. Not now, but in the future. I mean, it'd be a bit rude to say it now . . . we just met. But to answer your question "Why me?" meaning me, Sir Glossaryck of Terms, I have an answer for you: because you need me. I mean literally—this isn't an ego thing.

You see, magic is not like anything else: It has no language. No color. No shape. No smell. No feel. And for whatever reason, the universe has fabricated me, one Glossaryck, to take all the formless, odorless, colorless, flavorless abstraction of magic and present it to you like this.

fig.1e

Magic!

It's easier to understand what magic is, even "where" it is, if you imagine magic is the hobo stew that the universe swims in. Your wand lets you dip into that stew, but only just the surface.

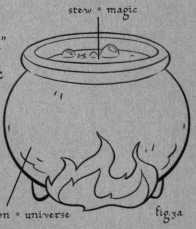

stew = magic

cauldron = universe   fig.3a

But You Just Wanna Learn Some Spells

Okay!

"Stop Being a Weirdy-Weird!"

Okay! Let's talk about your wand. You go first.

Hmmmm . . . okay. I get it. You don't know much about your wand. Maybe you're even confused by it. That's okay. Your wand is totally confusing. I mean, just look at it.

fig.3b

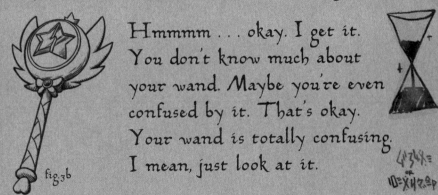

But don't get confused. Your wand isn't the important thing.

Your Book Is the Important Thing

Your Magic Instruction Book is an important catalogue of the role magic has played in your family. I also keep my socks and undie pants in it. If I'm here as a medium between magic and you, then the book is a way of recording how you experience the magic and how every princess before you experienced it. There are some amazing feats catalogued, as well as some real head-scratchers.

Take this entry from your grandmother Dirhhennia the Heaped. Her chapter is nothing but drawings of balls.

fig.3c

I mean, sure, she got creative; there
are 8-balls, eyeballs, string balls, big
balls, little balls. . . . But I mean . . .
it's all balls. Not a lot to present
to future generations. Her mother
argued there was something profound
    in her work, but we never could
        figure out what it was, and poor
        Dirhhennia was the only princess
    to be superseded by her younger
sister Crescenta the Eager, because
she was seen as unfit for the duties
of a queen.

But your grandmother Skywynne,
    Queen of Hours authored one of
    the most detailed and informative
    chapters. The spell on the next page,
    called Warnicorn Stampede, is a
    highlight of her chapter:

Here she has taken Warnicorn, the classic transformation spell . . .

INCANTATION DANCE

. . . and altered it with Stampede, multiplying the original warnicorn into a herd of warnicorns and then giving the herd locomotion. This was the final spell she created using the wand, before advancing to her role in the Magic High Commission, where she went on to create many exciting spells deviceless, or without a wand.

But You Just Want Me to Teach You to Be Deviceless

An excellent suggestion, but still dumb for two reasons:

> 1. I don't teach—not my bag. I'm only here to help you reach your potential.

> 2. Ya gotta walk before you can run (or something).

You'd Rather Just Run Now, Thanks

Okay. Thought you'd say that. Well, you can't run. . . . It's not the order of things. But! You can <u>sprint</u> . . . at least a bit. Remember the stew?

fig.4-c

Notice anything different? There, below the surface of the stew, are what I call the chunks. Your wand can only go so deep . . . but if you go inside yourself—"dip down"—you can get to those chunks. And you don't need your wand to do it; you simply do it. The wand only channels the magic; it is not in itself the magic.

Dipping down may happen without trying, but it's also something you can attempt. And it's the foundation for going deviceless. However, you can't learn without the proper tool, so for now, let's use this weird thing.

fig.36

The Magic High Commission
Call List

I created the beings of the Magic High Commission to provide Mewmans a means of understanding and interacting with magic. Together we oversee all the magic activity in the universe. Each council member is a representative for a particular realm of magic. They tend to despise me for every having created them. Kids, AMIRITE? To thank me for the gift of life, they make me attend stupid meetings I rarely have time for. Anyway, if you ever need to reach any of them, touch your mirror's Luthite Stone, then Salt Stone, then dial their "Mn" number. Keep this for reference in case of emergency.

I love you, *weird*

Glossaryck

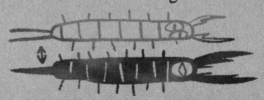

Magic Hand Mirror Movers

Fingala Magic Mirror Movers............................**Mn: D04-1-33-658**

Happy Mirror Movers.....................................**Mn: C99-3-11-098**

Magic High Commission

Glossaryck...................................**Mn: Z73-4-56-274**

Glossaryck—That's me, and the rest . . . well . . . what you know, you know.

Heckapoo.......................................**Mn: H15-2-23-717**

At some point it was clear that Mewmans would need a way to traverse the different dimensions of the multiverse, so I created Hekapoo and gave her the unique ability to be able to forge shears that can cut a rift between dimensions. Without Hekapoo's secret skill of forging dimensional scissors, all the dimensions would be infinitely separated, infinitely unaware of one another, basically. Except me, ya know, I mean, I can kinda go wherever.

Lekmet.....................**Mn: A11-1-34-237** (ask for Lekmet)

Lekmet is the most mysterious member of the Magic High Commission. I created him so that Mewmans would have an understanding of the impermanence of existence, but I'll be darned if anyone could understand him except his except his roommate, Rhombulus! He, Ominitraxis Prime, and I are all the original members of the MHC. His contribution to the commission must not be spoken, but I can be bribed for the info with the right kind of food.

St. Olga's Reform School for Wayward Princesses

"A Princess's Home Away from Home"

Mn: T21-6-65-865

Moon the Undaunted.........................**Mn: D08-3-44-642**

Not sure if you have the direct throne line? Moon the Undaunted, your mother, is the newest member of the Magic High Commission. She graduated to her role after exhibiting a mastery of the craft of magic, along with proving herself to be a trusted and principled leader of the people of Mewni. Her role on the commission is to oversee the relationship between Mewmans and magic.

Omnitraxis Prime.............................**Mn: B77-9-71-813**

Omnitraxis Prime has been around as long as anyone can remember; so long I almost don't remember making him. I think my original idea was I needed someone to be able to maintain the multiverse for Mewmans, and explain to them the delicate strands of spacetime. Turns out he's not much of an explainer, but he does a good job keep the multiverse from eating itself, I guess.

Rhombulus..........**Mn: A11-1-34-237** (ask for Rhombulus)

Rhombulus is an irritating man-baby. He's known for his emotional and reckless reactions to just about everything, as well as his hair-trigger instinct to freeze people in crystals. He's sorta the muscle of the commission. I turned his hands into thoughtful alligators in the hopes their intelligent thoughts would counteract his savage mind, but it didn't work. You know how every parent has a favorite? Well, they also have a least favorite ☹.

I Am Yvgeny Bulgolyubov
I Am Freelance Muscle
for Hire"
You Call Me Now:
Mn: Y78-32-456

DEALING WITH FAMILY
The Butterflies

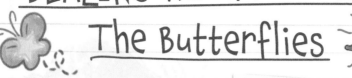

Moon Butterfly

This is my mom. They call her Moon the Undaunted . . . but they should probably call her Moon the Disappointed. Because, in general, she's pretty disappointed. I used

to be sad about it, but now I realize I'm just super good at disappointing her, so it's really like a skill, ya know? I know underneath it all she just wants me to make the family proud and be a good princess and ultimately a good queen. And super deep down, like way down, she's wearing some go-go boots that she got from a pole-dancing class under her petticoat. I think she taught me to question things, and I'm pretty sure that frustrates Glossaryck. She's also got these crazy magic powers that I never get to see her use, and she does it without a wand. Like she sticks out her hands and her eyes glow and she can move things and she grows these huge butterfly wings. Glossaryck calls it "dipping down." I did it once, but it was hard and it messed up my hair.

River Butterfly

Daddy! My dad's the best. He gets disappointed, too, but then he does the same thing that I do and then we laugh at each other and then he says, "Don't tell your mother." He comes from the Johansen clan. They are almost like people, but dirtier. My uncle Lump on my dad's side once ate a bear. Whole. My dad loves nature but he'll punch an eagle if it's a jerk eagle. He's a lot like me in that he will wrestle a clown even if he's not wearing clean underwear. He's cuddly and gives good hugs.

Stuff You Didn't Know about the Butterflies:

1. The royal lineage in Mewni is <u>matrilineal</u>, meaning the throne is handed down from mother to daughter. A man can only become royalty by marrying a queen or another member of the royal court.

2. My mom and dad actually met on the battlefield, when the Johansen clan was summoned from the woods to help the Mewni Guard fight off a great monster attack. It's one of the most historic battles in our history because Butterfly Castle was almost lost to the monsters.

3. When you're royalty, you end up with stuff that is excessive. We have a vacation cabin in a volcano. I've never been to it, because it's in a volcano. No one is sure it even exists, because it's in a volcano. But we have a vacation cabin in a volcano.

The Diazes

Angie Diaz

Angie is like my second mom, only she never gets mad at me! She's always so sweet and nice. One time she complained the monster fighting was getting too loud, so Marco and I saved up and bought her some headphones. :) She has a lot of hair! So much hair! I think she goes to work somewhere during the day, but . . . uh . . . not totally sure. Marco?

She teaches poetry at Echo Creek Community College. . . . Remember she wrote you that poem?

Oh, yeah! Duh! It went:

Our lives were so small and puny
till this angel arrived from Mewni.
Star is like a zany daughter
Who sometimes fills our home with water.

Rafael Diaz

Rafael cries a lot, and he listens to speed metal.

Hey! My dad is a sensitive artist, okay?

What? He's an artist?

YES. I didn't know that.

What did you think all of this art in the house was? The coyote with the long nose on the mantel? That crazy red thing on the lawn? The art shed?! Remember? We were trapped inside. . . . It was FULL of his art!

'kay, well, now I know. . . . Oh, yeah! One last thing. When Rafael takes off his shirt, it looks like he's wearing another shirt underneath made out of hair.

Five Facts about the Diazes

1. Rafael was born in Jalisco, Mexico, and Marco's grandma, Abuelita Linda, still lives there.

2. Angie and Rafael met at a café in Cleveland, Ohio.

3. Rafael collects old records.

4. Once a month Angie goes to the local comic book shop and competes in a Monster Trader card game tournament.

5. Rafael and Angie can usually be found cuddling on the couch, but sometimes they take breaks from doing that to shower and/or eat.

Parents: What to Do When They Send You Through a Dimensional Portal

Welp, if it hasn't happened yet, it probably will. At some point your parents are going to look at you and say, "We're sending you to another dimension."

Huh? That never happens. • ◉ • ◉ • ◉ •

You're thinking "That never happens," but you're wrong. It happened to me. It can happen to you.

I can't tell you how many times I've been powering through a Gulp/Slurp in front of the Stop-n-Slurp when I overhear some delinquent say, "What are my parents gonna do, send me to another dimension?" That question is always followed by the delinquent either pushing over a Dumpster or farting into a pay phone. Always under my breath I mumble, "Yes, hooligan . . . your parents WILL send you to another dimension."

• ◉ • ◉ • ◉ • ◉ • **Not on Earth . . .**

Yes, even on Earth. It's too late to talk prevention. It's gonna happen. So how do you deal? Here are some dos and don'ts from a young woman who's been there. There's a quiz later, so take notes.

- <u>Don't</u> yell and scream as they are loading your trunk onto the carriage that's about to take you to the new dimension. This will just reinforce their opinion that you're unhinged. The time for negotiations is over—you've been sanctioned. Remember, once they've decided, you can't stop it.

- <u>Do</u> feed the cat. You're gonna be gone a long time. Your parents have a kingdom to rule. Their servants have vants . . . to . . . uhhh . . . serv. No one is gonna take care of your cat. Look at a calendar, and count the days until the next holiday you'll be home for. Leave one scoop of kibble for each day you're gone. If it's over thirty days, get one of these:

It's a bit of an investment, but so is your love for your cat.

- <u>Don't</u> try to pack conservatively. It's important to bring every single thing you have with you. If you're traveling to Earth, I can give you some specific advice. For one, when you bring everything you have, people on Earth will see your stuff and they will know that you're in touch with the material world. You have your feet on the ground. Earth people (and people in a lot of dimensions) like solid, grounded people.

- Once you've arrived at your new home, <u>do</u> make it your own. It's daunting, but you're really obligated to use your magic to transform your environment (home, school, teachers, etc.) into something that works for you.

- <u>Don't</u> just piggyback on someone else's efforts. People are hospitable. Don't take advantage of their hospitality. If you've been a guest in your new home for a few days, and you haven't dramatically changed its architecture to look like your room back home, the person who lives in the house is gonna look at you and think, "All she does is use OUR architecture. When is she gonna get her own?" Is that who you want people to think you are—an architecture bum?

- <u>Don't</u> be an overachiever. It's alienating. Especially if you're an alien. Sometimes I'm tempted to clean up after myself, but I don't want to steal the limelight from Marco, the cleanest guy I know. If there are two overachievers in the house, where's the contrast? Be cool with taking the backseat and let your host shine.

Traveling with Your Parents to Another Dimension

Star gave my parents a spur-of-the-moment gift: a trip to another dimension. Specifically to Mewni (which is Star's home). It turned out to be the highlight of my parents' anniversary.

They loved your fanny packs, Marco.

Yes, the fanny packs came in very handy—helpful, just like I'd planned.

Which leads me to my point. To **our** point.

What <u>Not</u> to Pack When You Vacation in Mewni

I think the best way to illustrate this is to go through each person's bag and see what they actually packed.

We've gotten Marco's parents' permission. They think it's cute we're writing a book.

There's nothing cute about substandard emergency preparedness. Let's have a look.

Dad's Backpack:

My dad's backpack is a perfect example of what not to pack. None of the things in here would be helpful in an emergency.

Paintbrushes and Folding Easel:

Marco's dad is an artist. Instead of taking vacation photos, sometimes he likes to make vacation paintings.

Emergency Preparedness Rating: 0

I give this a "Thinking Outside the Box" rating of nine. (Four points for originality and five for the cool after-trip art show.)

Bubble Bath:

Useful if you stumble on a hidden hot spring and want to jazz up your already relaxing soak.

Emergency Preparedness Rating: 1

Massage Oil:

Have sore leg muscles from a serious day of exploring? Pull out the old massage oil and give your calves an oily rubdown.

Emergency Preparedness Rating: 2

Mom's Backpack:

My mom also has a bag full of things that would not be helpful in an emergency.

Summer Vacation Books:

Unless one of these pulp romance/ladies' literature books also comes with instructions on how to avoid getting eaten by giant human-guzzling plants in the Forest of Certain Death, they're pretty useless in an emergency.

Emergency Preparedness Rating: 1

Bikini:

This goes along with the bubble bath as something you should have with you when you find a mysterious hidden hot spring and want to have a relaxing soak.

Emergency Preparedness Rating: 2

Fruity Island Drink:

Preferably in a crazy coconut-pirate tiki glass.

Emergency Preparedness Rating: -10

I love crazy coconut pirates.

I'M NOT EVEN GOING TO TOUCH THIS ONE.

Marco's Fanny Pack:

Finally, a pack worth its weight in emergency preparedness gold. If you say the words "fanny pack" really fast over and over again, it sounds like you're saying "fan it back."

Space Blanket (Made for Two): It has an adorable Space Bear on it.

This blanket is fire-retardant. I specifically chose it as a special emergency addition to my fanny pack because I had a funny feeling that we might run into a multiheaded fire-breathing dragon or two on our vacation in Mewni.

You did not. You got me. I just liked the Space Bear.

Emergency Preparedness Rating: 8

Teensy Tiny Book of Knots: Tiny knots are soooo cool. Almost as cool as Space Bears.

I bought this teensy tiny book because I liked the cover. Star and I used it to tie up the multiheaded fire-breathing dragon that we thought had eaten my parents. But hadn't.

Emergency Preparedness Rating: 10

Sigh. That was a fun trip.

NON-DROWSY ANTIHISTAMINE

Dilemma Whistle:

Perfect for those moments when you're about to get devoured by a field of monsters whose headgear resembles beautiful flowers.

Emergency Preparedness Rating: 7

Meet the Pony Heads:

King Pony Head and His Thirteen Daughters

My family has had a long relationship with the Pony Heads. My dad and King Pony Head met as teens, when King Pony Head ran away from home. He escaped the Cloud Kingdom, hiding out in the Forest of Certain Death, where my dad was hunting Greebeasts. Because they both have one horn, my dad initially thought King Pony Head was a Greebeast and stalked him to a watering hole. As King Pony Head (then Prince Pony Head) was drinking, my dad jumped on him and they had a big tussle before my dad realized that he was wrestling a Pony Head, not a Greebeast.

They became fast friends, and he and my dad are close to this very day.

The Pony Heads are different from the Butterflies because they are <u>patrilineal</u>: the throne is handed down from the king to his firstborn son.

King and Queen Pony Head tried to have a boy, but the Pony Heads ended up with thirteen beautiful daughters.

I'D SAY MORE LIKE ONE OUTSTANDINGLY BEAUTIFUL DAUGHTER AND ELEVEN PLAIN DAUGHTERS WHO ARE BASICALLY JEALOUS OF THE BEAUTIFUL DAUGHTER'S BEAUTY . . . OH, AND ONE SWEET LI'L BABY.

Princess Pony Head

My bestie!

Princess Pony Head was born Lilacia Pony Head,

EWWW . . . DON'T TELL PEOPLE THAT!

but after her twelfth and final sister was born, it was obvious who the heir to the throne was gonna be, so her title became Princess Pony Head. Because we are both princesses, I don't have to use her title. We sorta call each other by our family names; I call her Pony Head and she calls me B-Fly.

YEAH, SO, MARCO, IF YOU'RE READING THIS, YOU ARE <u>NOT</u> ROYALTY AND YOU NEED TO ADDRESS ME BY MY TITLE, SON!

Azniss Pony Head

Azniss is the second-born Pony Head, and boy is she ever! She and Princess Pony Head don't really get along ← TOTES OBVI but I like Azniss. We're both HUGE fans of Mina Loveberry, Mewni's greatest defender. When we were little we'd play fight and always argue over who got to be Mina. As the second born, she'll be the commander in chief of the Pony Head Army one day, and she's already on her way to being a great warrior.

Angel Pony Head

Let this be a warning to parents: if you name your daughter Angel, she's never gonna be an angel. Angel Pony Head is a total troublemaker. She's basically a runaway who comes home every morning. She always has a different boyfriend, or two or three. When she's not on a motorcycle with her boyfriend(s), she likes to hang out in the dark behind buildings.

Khrysthalle Pony Head

Khrysthalle can usually be found looking at herself in the family reflecting pool.

MORE LIKE SHE HOGS IT SO NO ONE ELSE CAN USE IT!

I heard she's the most BEAUTIFUL of all the Pony Heads. DON'T EVEN.

Sometimes it seems like she's stuck there. A couple of times I've gone in and she's fallen asleep in the pool. I don't think that's safe.

Jan-Jan Pony Head

Jan-Jan knows how to party. She says she has a mohawk, but you can't really tell because all ponies look like they have a mohawk. As the fifth born, she'll be the party ambassador for the kingdom, and she's perfectly suited for it.

amanda . . . the unloved
e child. If there's a dead
in any family, it's the
ddle child.

id Shinda Pony Head

Th   s. I heard that when they were born the king was super excited, because he always wanted to have a twin daughter vocal group. The girls have no real musical talent, but that didn't stop the king from paying for them to record <u>2 Hearts 4 U</u>, an . . . uh . . . interesting album featuring the twins singing duets. When the album didn't sell, he had it "installed" in every household in the Cloud Kingdom of the Pony Heads.

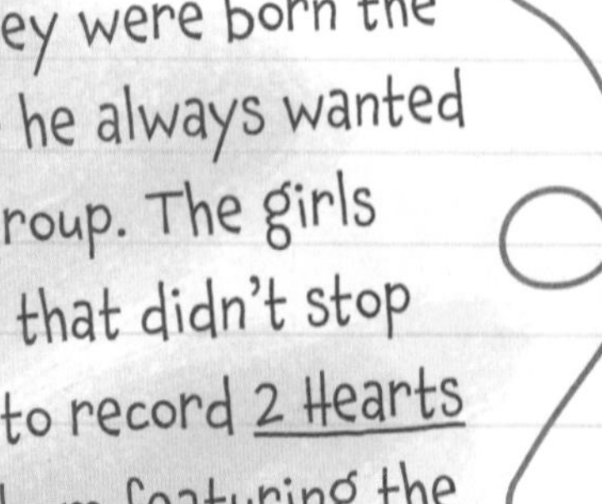

I HAVEN'T EVEN HEARD IT. . . . I CAN'T. I CAN'T EVEN STAND TO LISTEN TO SHONDA SING IN THE SHOWER.

131

Hor~~rible~~

Unfo...
the o...
without...
inevitable...
but then it n...

Teta Pony Head

Her oats are always eaten. Her homework is al~~ways~~ done. She's never missed a day of school. She's a model Pony Head. But no one knows where she is. "Has anybody seen Teta?" is the most commonly asked question at Castle Pony Head.

I JUST SAW HER YESTERDAY . . . I THINK.

Everyone says, "I just saw her yesterday," but when pressed for details on that, no one can quite remember if it was yesterday, or the day before, or the day before. . . . But I guess as long as her homework is done, nbd?

Chezna Pony Head

Chezna is the least Pony Head Pony Head. When she came of age, the first thing she did with her Out-Coming money was to have her horn filed off and get a body implant. She'd just rather be a horse. I love Chezna, but she's always asking to give me horsey rides, and it's a little scary because she doesn't really know how to work her legs just yet.

Whistine Pony Head

Whistine "Old Baby" Pony Head. Poor thing, she thought she was gonna be the baby, but then— SURPRISE—Pranciss was born and stole the position from her. You almost made it, Whistine. Anyway, Whistine turned out pretty good. She definitely looks up to Pony Head, and sorta models herself after her eldest sister.

Baby Pranciss Pony Head

By far the MOST adorable. Just look at her.

OMG, SO CUTE! I WANNA SMASH HER FACE WITH MY HORN!

She's such a sweet little thing. We will have to wait and see who she turns out to be. . . .

EWW! WHAT IS THIS MESS? ↘

Quiz of the Lands in Mewni*

*See "Star and Marco's (and Pony Head's) Map of the Dimensions" for more Mewni information.

1. The kingdom of the Waterfolk has three water parks that Mewmans can visit. Each water park is themed like one of the three levels of Mewni—the Cloud Kingdom, the Groundlands, and the Underworld—with water rides named after royalty from each one. Which water ride would you find in the Underworld-themed water park?

a. The Tom: a crazy waterslide with seventeen loops that turns you upside down and sideways and scrambles your brain like merman eggs. Plus, the water is superheated to burn-your-face-off hot and leaves weird red spots on your skin for hours afterward.

b. The River: a relaxing river ride where you float in inner tubes and hit pop-up cardboard cutouts of monsters (placed at strategic points) with your paddle.

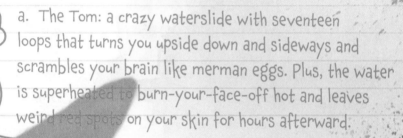

c. The Marco: not really a ride. You put on a red hoodie, stand in the baby pool, and have someone pour water over your head with a pail.

Ew, babies pee in the baby pool.

d. The Moon: an enclosed waterslide whose ceiling is covered in magical constellations so that you feel like you're sliding through the night sky.

135

2. Which castle did I, Star Butterfly, grow up in?

a. Castle Avarius

b. Castle Johansen

c. Butterfly Castle

d. Castle Pony Head

3. Marco and I went on vacation to Mewni with Marco's parents for their anniversary. This was their first trip to another dimension, and they had a lot of fun. Even if we all Which of these places (that exists in Mewni) almost died did they get to see on their visit? there. At least three different times.

a. The Bounce Lounge, where they got to dance the night away to a set by DJ Jump-Jump

b. Quest Buy, where they used a magical gift card to buy matching tracksuits

c. The Amethyst Arcade, where they played video games and ate corn dogs until they both felt sick to their stomachs

d. The Forest of Certain Death, where they almost got eaten by monsters, like, three different times

4. There was only one drive-in carriage theater in Mewni, and it closed down recently due to a gorbally infestation. But before that happened, Pony Head and I used to go there all the time to eat big fake turkey-leg candy and see Shastaspearan plays put on by some of Mewni's best actors. Which of these plays did we <u>not</u> see? (You will know it because it did <u>not</u> take place in one of the lands in Mewni.)

a. Momeo and Ruliet in the Forest of Certain Death

b. Julio Cesario Goes to the Underworld

c. A Late Winter's Nap in the Cloud Kingdom

d. Hammyletto Visits Earth

INTERDIMENSIONAL RELATIONSHIPS

Interdimensional Dating

These are some interviews I did as research.
I wanted to know from other people what dating across
dimensions was like before I attempted it for myself.

On the outside it looks
pretty easy, but after
talking to Janna and
Skullzy, I learned some
really important stuff . . .
like always having a good
dictionary on hand.

Star: For the record, what is your name?

Miss Skullnick: My name is Margaret Skullnick—but that's
still _Miss_ Skullnick to you, Star.

S: Where do you hail from?

MS: I used to be a normal human being from Earth
until you turned me into a troll with your magical
wand thingy. Not a big fan of the giant teeth;
makes it hard to bite my nails. But the heavy-duty
superhuman troll strength isn't bad.

S: Soooooo . . . tell me about the pitfalls of interdimensional dating.

MS: Oh, okay . . . Well, I used to play regular old darts on Tuesdays with some of the other ladies from Echo Creek Academy: Jenny Minerva, the assistant gym coach; Delilah Batterbrook, the assistant school nurse; and Fanny Tuttertall, the assistant lunch lady. But since "the change" they won't let me play with them anymore.

They say I cheat at darts. Well, I'm here to tell you that it's not cheating. It's just this heavy-duty superhuman troll strength of mine. . . . It doesn't know its own strength.

S: Um, I said interdimensional <u>dating</u>, not interdimensional <u>darts</u>. . . .

MS: Oh my, now don't I feel silly! What you really want to know is the intimate details of my relationship with Emmitt, the monster who left me out to dry on a laundry line.

S: Eek. That must've been painful.

MS: Well, my last boyfriend left me on the dock . . . which isn't any better . . . but at least J knew he was leaving. With Emmitt, we had a real language barrier. He did a lot of grunting and gesticulating—and J'm not a real whiz at running charades, so when he left me—J _think_ he left me, it was kind of hard for me to tell—J didn't get a whole lot of closure. A friend said J should get a Monster to English dictionary, but, frankly, J didn't want to spend the money.

S: What drew you to your interdimensional boyfriend Emmitt?

MS: Jt wasn't just because he had abs of steel. He was a nice guy. Always held the door open for me—he only closed it in my face once. He was a real romantic: brought me flowers he'd chewed the buds off of; took me to the racetrack, where we bet on schnauzers; sold my shoes to a homeless man . . . while J was wearing them.

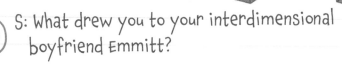

S: So you don't regret your interdimensional
dating experience?

MS: There were good times and bad times. I wouldn't
trade them. But if I had it to do all over again, I'd
spend the $5.98 and buy that stupid dictionary.

Why was Miss Skullnick talking about darts?

I don't know, Marco. That interview almost makes
me feel bad for Miss Skullnick.

The lady who put you in detention?

Yeah, I know. But they did make me mayor of detention
and I only have Miss Skullnick to thank for that.

It's an honorary title.

I could get voted in for life. You never know.

Then I remembered
that Janna
interdimensional
dated, so I figured
I oughta get the
scoop from someone
more my age, but
honestly . . . Janna's bananas.

Star: Let's talk about interdimensional dating. Tell me about Bernardo, the skeleton you met because of me.

Janna: So I met Bernardo when Star took over our class field trip. We were originally supposed to spend the day at the Echo Creek Museum of Paper Clips, but Star talked Miss Skullnick into letting us go somewhere way more exciting.

S: Yup, just keep saying "Star" like I'm not even here. Or like I'm not Star interviewing you.

J: Well, that's how the class ended up in the Dimension of Wonders and Amazements. It was pretty cool. But the coolest part was definitely meeting Bernardo.

I don't believe in love at first sight, but he

was so confident. Like he knew he was cool. And Marco wasn't ready to date someone as fierce as me (sorry, Marco).

S: Cool! What was your first date like?

: It was pretty romantic. We went to an underground crypt where everyone totally knew who he was. We heard a dope band called Rip Up the Macabre—they were kind of ska and punk and dead, all at the same time. My body is an occult temple, so I never touch anything harder than a cranberry juice cocktail when I'm out at a club. Bernardo was supercool about it. He says skeletons don't really drink, either. Which was probably not true, but I appreciated him trying to make me feel comfortable.

S: Are you guys gonna go out again?

J: Are you crazy? NO WAY.

S: Really? But it seemed like you liked each other. . . .

J: FINAL ANSWER.

S. Okay . . . uh, thanks.

And <u>then</u> Marco wanted me to interview Jackie-Lynn
Thomas with questions he had written (which were very
Marco-centric) . . . and I was like, "That's not interdimensiona
dating when you're from the same dimension," but he
promised to make me more
triangle food . . . YUM . . . and so
I said I would . . . but I honestly
don't think this interview should
be included in the book.

Star: So . . . Jackie-Lynn
        Thomas . . . expert
skateboarder and owner of the second most
beautiful eyes at Echo Creek Academy (number one
are Oskarrrrr's . . . drool) . . . um . . . yeah . . . tell
me about what you are looking for in a . . . man?

Jackie-Lynn
    Thomas: The last guy I had a crush on was this
really cute guy from skate camp last
summer (he was really nice), and so
he'd been, like, totally on my mind a lot.

S: You just said "had."

JLT: I did?

S: Yeah, you did. Why did you say "had"? Like you don't
have a crush on the guy from skate camp anymore?

JLT: Well, I guess I might like someone else now.

S: Um, now back to my personally prepared questions. Tell me about your relationship with Marco Diaz.

JLT: My relationship with Marco is really confusing, I guess. I mean, if I really think about it, I've always kinda known that maybe Marco likes me . . . as more than a friend. I mean, he started sending me those anonymous kitten pics—which I totally knew were from him—but I think because I really valued him as a friend and didn't want to ruin our friendship, I kinda ignored the signs. Plus, cute guy from skate camp last summer, ya know?

S: Here is my next thoroughly researched question: do you like Marco Diaz as more than a friend? Check yes or no—wait, I wasn't supposed to read that part out loud.

JLT: You're funny, star.

S: Hahahahahaha. But seriously. Do you like Marco Diaz as more than a friend?

JLT: Not until we were at your sleepover party and we played Truth or Punishment, with that awful box that forces you to tell the truth. And when it asked Marco who he had a crush on . . . well, he said me. Which totally blew my mind . . . but not really. . . .

JLT: And for the first time, i really looked at him, ya know? Like totally stared him in the eyes and saw down deep into his soul . . . and he was, like, uh, really cute. Adorable even. with his little mole and his saucy brown eyes. And he really, really liked me. Like, for real. And the cute guy from skate camp was only a friend, because nothing ever happened between us, so i had nothing to feel bad about in discovering that maybe i kinda liked Marco, too.

wow, i guess my feelings for Marco aren't as confusing as i thought they were. i mean, i definitely have a crush on him now, too. which is crazy. To think that Marco and i both have a crush on each other at the same time. i'm really glad we talked this out. Thanks, star.

S: uh . . .

Interview end.

M + JL

Marco's Tip for Asking Out Chicks:
Don't

Take it from a guy who never gets what he wants . . . especially when it comes to dating the girl he has a crush on:

Cough, cough, Jackie-Lynn Thomas, cough, cough.

Just become a monk. It's safer. Just kidding.

I have tried many techniques in the arena of dating. Most of them don't work. Here are a few of them.

The Nod

This technique has been in my arsenal for over a decade—basically, as long as I've known Jackie-Lynn Thomas. From the outside, it looks very simple, but trust me when I say that there's a lot of subtlety to this move.

It takes a steady heart and an even steadier head—otherwise, if you're not careful, you can end up looking like an out-of-control bobblehead.

Step 1. Freeze. You've just seen the girl of your dreams skateboarding down the hallway.

Keep going. There's more than one step, duh.

<u>Step 2.</u> Unfreeze. This is not freeze tag. You have, like, fiv
seconds until the girl of your dreams comes into range.

<u>Step 3.</u> Lean. The key is to find a locker or a water
fountain or a wall to lean against so that you look super
casual when the girl of your dreams notices you standing
there.

<u>Step 4.</u> Make eye contact. It's important to direct the nod
at the right person. If you don't lock gazes, you might end
up nodding at the wrong person. Which can be awkward if
it's someone you don't know or wish you didn't know.

<u>Step 5.</u> Nod. No explanation needed.

<u>Step 6.</u> Wait for a reply nod from the girl of your dream
Hopefully you get one, but if you don't, it's A-okay. You
can try again the next day.

<u>Step 7.</u> Turn into a
puddle of goop. The girl
of your dreams is gone
and the fear you've
been holding inside can
finally be let out.

The Kit-Pic Text Technique

I like to use this technique when I feel like reaching out but I don't want to actually put myself out there. It's a little research heavy and you can spend a lot of time looking for the right kitten picture to match your mood. It's like going down a kit-pic wormhole—you never know what you're going to find.

Step 1. Take out your phone. This is where the battle will take place.

Step 2. Find a kit-pic. Like I said, this can take time. It has to be purrfect.

Step 3. Text the kit-pic to the girl of your dreams. This is the trickiest part. It can take a while to work up the right amount of courage to get the job done.

Step 4. Sit back and let the LOLs roll in.

The Truth or Punishment Box Technique
(Not recommended)

Sometimes Star has a sleepover party and invites the girl of your dreams. And sometimes you get roped into playing a game that Pony Head brought that, at first, sounds terrible and is not what you want to be doing—but then Star forces you to play it anyway and it's even worse than you thought it would be. And you end up, maybe, um, saying some stuff that you really didn't want to say, um, <u>out loud</u>, just so you don't, uh, die, and, yeah . . . it sucks.

<u>Step 1.</u> Just say no. This is almost impossible to do. No one will let you quietly walk away from this sleepover party game.

<u>Step 2.</u> Grin and bear it. You are now playing a sleepover party game with the girl of your dreams. You want her to think you're cool . . . so act cool.

<u>Step 3.</u> Be direct. The Truth or Punishment Box does not accept anything but the truth. If you answer its questions with an outright lie or even a half-truth, it will do awful things to you and your fellow game players (including the girl of your dreams).

Step 4. Accept it. The Truth or Punishment Box <u>will</u> force you to say the name of your crush. Out loud. When she is sitting right next to you.

The Honesty Technique

When all else fails and the
Naysaya on your neck forces
you to do it . . . just be
honest. I know it's really scary,
but if you don't ask for what
you want . . .
Like a date with Jackie-Lynn
Thomas

Star's right. Like a date with
Jackie-Lynn Thomas . . . you'll probably never get it.

<u>Step 1.</u> Find the girl of your dreams. Make sure she's alone.

<u>Step 2.</u> Take a deep breath. You are about to
do something you don't wanna do, but you do.

<u>Step 3.</u> Open your mouth.

<u>Step 4.</u> Tell her how you really feel. There may be some
false starts at first, but after a few seconds of opening
and closing your mouth, the right words will come out.

<u>Step 5.</u> Hope for the best. You don't know how the girl of
your dreams will respond, but at this point, you've done all
you can do. The ball is in her court.

So just to clarify: asking for what you want can sometimes
suck . . . but sometimes it doesn't suck.

Date, Marry, or Make Disappear Forever

This is a fun Earth game I learned when I had a sleepover party with Janna, Pony Head, StarFan13, and Jackie-Lynn Thomas. We play a version in Mewni called Court, Betroth, or Sell, but it's kinda the same idea. I thought it would be fun to play this with Marco and Pony Head, since even though we are writing this book to combat BOREDOM . . . I am getting kinda bored of this chapter.

I'm down. Just don't force me to have to choose between marrying Tom and Miss Skullnick. Tom and I are working on being friends right now and it would be weird, and Skullnick is . . . let's just say she's intense.

Pony Head, who would you rather . . .

Date, Marry, or Make Disappear Forever?

☐ Alfonzo ☐ Marco *Hey! Not fair.* ☐ Mina Loveberry

THAT'S EZ. EARTHTURD WOULD DISAPPEAR.

Fine by me.

DATE MINA LOVEBERRY, CUZ SHE IS CRAY-Z. DEF NOT THE SETTLING-DOWN TYPE. I GUESS I GOTTA MARRY ALFONZO

I think he might already be married.

IT'S JUST A <u>GAME</u>, EARTHTURD.

My turn. Pony Head, who would you rather . . .
Date, Marry, or Make Disappear Forever?

☐ Spikeballs EW   ☐ Toffee EW, EW, EW   ☐ Ludo AS IF!

EW, MARCO DIAZ, THESE ARE ALL TERRIBLE.

Just answer the question, Pony Head.

Those are all pretty bad, Marco.

WHAT EVZ . . . DATE SPIKEBALLS, MARRY TOFFEE, DISAPPEAR LUDO. EW.

You didn't choose. You just went in a row.

UH, YOU SAID CHOOZ. I DID.

Sorry, Marco, she did choose.

Now it's my turn again. Marco, who would you rather . . .
Date, Marry, or Make Disappear Forever?

☐ Jackie-Lynn Thomas   ☐ Pony Head   ☐ Janna

GUYZ, I CHOOZ DISAPPEARING FOR ME.

My turn, not yours.

This is easy. Date . . . Pony Head.

EW! NO . . . OVER MY DEAD PONY HEAD BODY.

That doesn't make any sense. Marry . . . no surprises here . . .
Jackie-Lynn Thomas . . . and, um, Janna would disappear.

Not where I thought you would go with this one, Marco.

Janna would probably be down for disappearing. It's spooky
and she likes spooky stuff. She's weird like that.

LET ME DO YOU, B-FLY. . . .

DATE, MARRY, OR MAKE DISAPPEAR FOREVER

☐ TOM   ☐ OSKAR   ☐ OSKAR-KHESTRA

This one doesn't seem right to me.

QUIET, EARTHTURD. MY TURN!

This is an easy one. . . . Date Oskar-khestra, marry . . .
Oskar . . . and make Tom disappear forever.

That was a fun game. We should play Court,
Betroth, or Sell now. NO! NO!

Ya know, I don't think you guys have ever agreed on
anything before. . . .

Not agreeing.

NO WAYZ.

Okay . . . but it does kinda seem like you guys are
agreeing. . . . SEE YA LATERZ, B-FLY.

I gotta go do some homework.

Well, that was a weird end to that game. You can
ignore our choices and go through and make your
154   own for each one.

Doctor Marco, PhD, Presents:

Interdimensional Dating Psychology 101—Overview

After Star interviewed Jackie-Lynn Thomas for me, I sorta felt like I should return the favor and ask Oskar a few questions. Okay, that's not wholly the truth. . . . She actually _made_ me do it. She gave me a list of questions, and frankly, they were so obviously Star-like, I felt it was my duty, as a friend, to change them. I started thinking . . . what would Doctor Marco, PhD, do in this situation?

Doctor Marco, PhD, would use . . . _psychology._

It is a perfect technique to level the dating field and make it safe to walk across. I found my subject at rest in his natural habitat: his mobile music studio, aka the front seat of his car. Here is a transcript of the session that took place.

Doctor Marco, PhD: Hey.

OSKAR: HEY.

DMPhD: Mind if I get in?

O: SURE, MARCO.

DMPhD: For the record, please state your name.

O: WHAAA?

DMPhD: Why don't you tell me about your childhood?

O: WHY?

DMPhD: We can skip that one. Think fast: girlfriend or music? Say the first thing that comes into your head.

O: GENE . . .

DMPhD: Hmmm . . . very interesting. Note to self: subject is obsessed with his ferret.

O: NO, DUDE, HE'S SITTING ON YOUR SHOULDER.

DMPhD: Ah . . . let's move on then. I'm gonna read
you something now.

J: YOU'RE BEING KINDA WEIRD, MARCO.

DMPhD: Just bear with me. "I don't have to follow
your rules. I'm gonna live in my car at the
school." Tell me about these lyrics.

O: UH, MY MOM AND I GOT IN A FIGHT.
SO I WROTE A SONG ABOUT IT.

DMPhD: Subject clearly has mother issues.

O: WHAT ARE YOU TALKING ABOUT?

DMPhD: Moving on . . . Do you know Star Butterfly?

O: SURE, SHE'S COOL.

DMPhD: Subject referred to Star as "cool."
Still moving on . . . Let's do some free
associations. Polar Bear . . .

O: AM I SUPPOSED TO SAY SOMETHING?

DMPhD: You could say "cold" or "snow" or "ice," maybe.

O: ICE.

DMPhD: Do you have a girlfriend? 'Cause I think Star—

(Session is interrupted by the arrival of "The Rageaholic
Demon Prince," aka Star's ex-boyfriend, Tom.) 157

Tom: I don't think you want to say what you were just going to say, Marco.

DMPhD: Tom, this is unexpected.

T: I put a little side curse on you. Nothing as fancy as the Naysaya one, but just as effective. It lets me know whenever you mention Star.

DMPhD: But I talk about Star all the time.

T: I have someone monitoring the line for that very reason. (To Oskar) By the way, we haven't been introduced.

DMPhD: Oskar, this is Star's demon ex-boyfriend, Tom

O: OH, COOL. I'M OSKAR AND THAT'S GENE THE FERRET.

T: Gene, the pleasure is all mine. I've heard very good things about you from my minions.

DMPhD: So . . . <u>Tom</u> . . . Oskar and I were sorta in the middle of something.

T: Oh, don't mind me. I'm fine back here with all these keytars. Carry on.

DMPhD: Um . . . so . . . where was I?

T: Ice.

DMPhD: This is my session, Tom.

T: Of course. My lips will stay zipped.

O: UH. THIS IS WEIRD.

DMPhD: Okay . . . my next question—

T: Oskar. May I call you Oskar?

O: SURE, DUDE.

T: Oskar. I know people who know people who <u>know</u> people in the music biz. I hear you make tunes, and I'd love to introduce you—

DMPhD: Stop highjacking my session, Tom. I'm gonna tell Star—

T: You're not going to tell Star.

159

DMPhD: I am too.

T: Are not.

DMPhD: Yeah, uh-huh, I am.

T: No way.

DMPhD: Yes way.

O: UH, LITTLE BROMANCE DUDES, I GOTTA JET. SEE YA ON THE FLIP SIDE.

(Oskar leaves car.)

DMPhD: Now look what you did.

T: What I did?

DMPhD: Bromance? I don't even know what he's talking about.

T: Yeah, that comment was totally off base . . . right, Gene? Because if I was bromancing you, Marco . . . if I was, you would know it.

OUR BODIES, OUR SPELLS

Mewberty vs. Puberty—
Star and Marco Explain

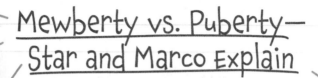

Stages of
Mewberty

MEH
fig. 1

ADULT

fig. 4

BAC

fig. 2

HEART
COCOON

fig. 3

Sooooo . . .
when girls
reach a certain
age on Mewni,
they . . . uh . . . go
through this thing. . . .
It's sorta major. You
know how when you're little you look at boys and
you're kinda like "meh" (fig.1), but then one day you
look at them and it's like they are all made out of
bacon (fig. 2), and it's like you've never eaten, you're
so hungry, and the only food you want is bacon?

162

So you try to hide out, but that doesn't work and you basically cocoon in a locker or wherever (fig.3), but then you blossom into a flower-alien butterfly creature (fig.4). The problem is, boys are everywhere, so basically you gotta, like, cocoon all the boys into this purple stuff made from hearts and you grow wings and extra arms. It lasts a few hours and hopefully at the end everyone is okay, and the cool thing is you get to keep the little wings!

This makes no sense whatsoever. . . . Is this scientific?

I had to improvise, okay? And, hey, I may have grown wings, but your body-changing stuff was way crazier than mine. Maybe we should talk about that?

Talk about my changing body? No way are we talking about that! All the things my body may or may not do are strictly private!

EW, gross! I meant changing body as in when your arm became a monster arm and when you grew a giant beard, Marco.

Oh, those kinds of changes—great transition, Star!

163

When Not to Skim, or Oops, What Happened to Marco?

I don't always have time to read my spells before I cast them, but when I do I'm always glad I did. Not the case with Releaseo Demonius Infestica. Had I read the entire description of that spell, I probably would have used something different to mend Marco's broken arm.

Sometimes, when I'm in a hurry, I sorta "skim" my spell book.

Skimming is a reading technique I learned at Echo Creek Academy, where you read for key words and ignore everything else. Here's how the Releaseo Demonius Infestica spell appears in my book. I've gone ahead and highlighted the key words I read before I cast it. As you can see, the other words were sorta important, too:

Releaseo Demonius Infestica:

To be cast in the rare instance when you need to heal a broken bone AND infect the host with a demonic tentacle virus.

STAGES:

1. Bone heals.

2. Virus braids itself into the host's skeletal system.

3. Healed bone "hatches" into a sentient tentacle being.

4. Tentacle being turns evil, implants negative and destructive thoughts into the mind of the host, causing him to behave in erratic, possibly lethal ways.

5. Tentacle being eventually takes over control of the host.

6. Host dies.

Not dissimilar to when I took it upon myself to grow Marco a beard. Here's how that spell appears in my book, again, highlighting only the key words that jumped out at me:

Sparkledust Beard Expand

To be cast in the rare instance when you need to stimulate beard growth in a host AND suffocate and destroy the host with said beard.

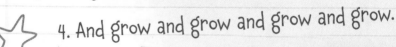

STAGES:

1. Beard grows.

2. Beard continues to grow.

3. And grow and grow and grow.

4. And grow and grow and grow and grow.

5. Host dies.

Foods Teens Need for Growing and Stuff

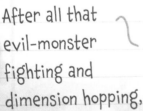

After all that evil-monster fighting and dimension hopping, a princess can really work up an appetite. When I'm starving and need to feed my body some healthy foods, I call on Marco to cast Earth magic on my tum-tum with his Super Awesome Nachos . . . AND he's agreed to share the secrets of this magic with you!

Most family recipes are handed down over generations. But no one in my family knows how to cook. Like, no one. So I took it upon myself to start the legacy of family recipes with my Super Awesome Nachos.

My nachos have a few key layers: pre-seasoned chips, frijoles de la olla (Spanish for "beans from the pot"), cheese, guacamole, pico de gallo (Spanish for "beak of the rooster"), and fresh jalapeños.

Marco's Super Awesome Nachos

Here's what you will need:

Chips

Bag of corn tortilla chips

Juice of 1 lime

1¼ tsp cumin

1 tsp paprika

1 pinch cinnamon

1 pinch chili powder (Careful!)

Pico de Gallo

Store-bought will do the trick.

Frijoles de la Olla

P.S. Until you're a master nachoist like me, make sure your parents are around to help you cook.

Put a can of pinto beans in a pot with a tablespoon of olive oil. Bring them to a boil, then reduce to a simmer for about 10 minutes, adding salt and pepper to taste.

Guacamole

(or sub with store-bought if you're lazy)

2 avocados, cut into small cubes

Juice of 1 lime

1 tomato, chopped

1 jalapeño, seeded, diced

Salt, pepper to taste

Mix these ingredients together in a bowl about 20 minutes before serving, then cover and refrigerate.

Cheese Sauce

(No shortcuts . . . you MUST not be lazy about this.)

4 tbsp butter

6 tbsp flour or cornstarch

¼ cup milk

1 block soft cheese, shredded (pepper jack, soft cheddar, etc.)

1 pinch chili powder (Careful!)

Prepare the Cheese Sauce

To make the cheese sauce, you're gonna start by making a roux, which is a French word. It's a base that gives sauces a nice thickness. Melt the butter and whisk in the flour. Cook until it starts to bubble, then lower the heat. Whisk in the milk and allow mixture to return to bubbling before adding in the shredded cheese slowly, bit by bit, as it melts.

The Chips

Place chips in a paper bag, and squeeze lime juice into the bag. Sprinkle spices onto the chips, then close the bag and shake to coat.

Combine

Pour chips onto an oven-safe platter in a couple of layers. Then ladle the beans and some bean broth onto the chips. Sounds gross but it's amazing. Trust. Place the platter in a preheated oven at 375 degrees for about 10 minutes to warm the chips and bind them with the bean juices.

Remove the platter from the oven and generously ladle the cheese sauce over them. Cover with the cold guacamole, pico de gallo, and chopped jalapeños. It's important the fresh ingredients are cold to add contrast between the hot chips/beans/cheese layers below. Serve this delicious mess immediately.

Now that you're done, do the world a favor and DON'T take a picture of your food! No one wants to see that.

(Pssst . . . great with watermelon agua fresca or iced horchata!)

FASHION

Dress for Warfare and/or the Club!

You never know when you're going to be faced with combat AND partying in the same half hour. So I just dress for both: kicking monster butt and then rolling right into the Bounce Lounge to meet Pony Head for a set by DJ Jump-Jump.

I vote red hoodie and jeans for any situation you find yourself in. They are both comfortable and impervious to monster and spell-casting goo.

Some people we know—but who will remain nameless—have tried to fight monsters in their cheerleading uniforms. But even when pom-poms come with booty-shaking dance moves, they are <u>not</u> a part of a good combat ensemble.

I don't think Brittney and the other cheerleaders were actually trying to fight monsters. They were more like running away from them.

Here are some of my favorite outfits and when to wear them:

This is a good dress for when you've frozen time and didn't realize that once you'd frozen it, Father Time was gonna get all excited about finally being free from his giant hamster wheel of Progress and refuse to unfreeze it again.

Why it's perfect:

- Cactus headgear is great for storing water, which can come in handy when time is frozen and you need a quick drink.

- Octopuses are good problem solvers. They like to use tools.

- Rhinoceros-horn shoes are good for hanging out in the Plains of Time. They have special bubblegum treads on the bottom that adhere to stuff, which is especially important when you're wading in the Pocketwatch Rapids and don't want to get washed away.

Want to hit the Bounce Lounge, but then be down to spar with St. O's robot security detail when they're after your best friend and the dimensional scissors she may or may not have borrowed? This is the outfit for that.

Why it's perfect:

- I call this my Edgar dress, because Edgar is the name of the little bear on the front.
- There's no AC in the Bounce Lounge. It's in the clouds. BUT you can still pit-out your dress sleeves when the dance floor is bumpin', so I always go sleeveless when I go dancing. Plus, I like to show off my wand-wielding arms. Later, when St. O's fuzz comes down to get my bestie, I can easily roll into action mode with no puffy sleeves to get in the way.
- Even though this is a light dress, there's still room to stow a sword, and it's hardly noticeable. Look closely—can you see the sword?

Sometimes you need an outfit that tells the world you are in charge—that you can handle any situation, no matter how out-of-this-world crazy it gets. This is not that outfit. This outfit is for when you have to admit that maybe Miss Skullnick was right.

Maybe the class would have been better off at the Echo Creek Museum of Paper Clips.

Why it's perfect:

Leg warmers are like minidresses for your feet. They keep your legs warm and protect your shins when you are kicking someone in the head. Star, you shouldn't kick people in the head.

I'd never kick a person in the head. Only a jerky-jerk monster.

- I love these blue-striped tights because they were a gift from my dad. They're made of manticore skin, which allows them to breathe and is also impervious to blades and claws. Also, the manticore is unharmed in the process, so they're kinda eco.

- It's durable. It survived my Mewberty transformation.

There are dresses that can rea[lly]
take a beating and keep on tick[ing]

I think it's "take a licking,"
and I think they're talking
about watches.

Well, this dress is kind of like [a]
watch, Marco. It's very reliab[le]
and I don't have to wind it.

Your dress is __still__ not like a watch[.]

It has a lot of freedom of movement, so I can do crazy
monster-fighting moves like cartwheel tentacle kicks
and roundhouse antler punches.

Why it's perfect:

- The spider necklace may look like
  bling to the naked eye, but it's a real live spider!

- The puffy sleeves are actually giant pockets made
  up of a whole bunch of mini-pockets. I once let a
  family of flying squirrels stay in the right sleeve for
  a few weeks, which turned into a few months and
  then a year. You know, they may still be living there.
  I haven't checked in a while.

- This dress is like a watch because when I wear it, I
  know that it's "having fun o'clock" and that "going
  on an adventure hour" is fast approaching.

Okay. The dress is like a watch. I give up.

Marco has asked me to include his karate gi because he says that it's multifunctional and great for the dojo, birthday parties, or monster bloodbaths. I say from a distance it looks like long underwear or jammies, so maybe the gi doesn't have the versatility he thinks.

Allow me to explain why it works:

The further you are in your karate learning, the more versatility you have in belt choices. I'm a red belt, so I can choose white, yellow, orange, or green belts because I have them in my closet. I got the white belt when I was nine so it may be a snug fit. :(

- Tie-on white headbands are great for keeping the sweat out of your eyes when you're fighting monsters, and when you're surfing the mosh pit at the Scum Bucket.

Star may be the expert, but I've been to a few dimensions myself, and one thing is universal: women love a man in uniform. The more sophisticated woman will see the gi and not confuse it for long underwear or jammies. She will see the elegant power of a spiritual warrior.

Or a guy who's given up and is wearing his bathrobe out of the house?

The monster will see the gi and cower as he recognizes the warrior's status as a master of martial arts.

177

WELL, FOR ME, IT'S ALL ABOUT THE NECK HOLE. SEE, PONY HEADS DON'T HAVE A NEED FOR CLOTHES, E-TURD, SO WE ATTRACT MATES AND DISTRACT ENEMIES BY EMITTING COLORFUL STARS FROM OUR NECK HOLES.

Uhhhhh . . . I think I'm gonna be sick.

That does make sense. Clothes are kind of overrated when you don't have a body.

THE STARS ARE AS ATTRACTIVE AS THEY ARE DANGEROUS. I'M BASICALLY LIKE ONE OF THOSE BAD VILLAIN GIRLS IN THE SPY MOVIES WHO USES HER BEAUTY TO BE LIKE, "OH, LOOK AT ME," BUT THEN SECRETLY IT'S LIKE, "WHA! SURPRISE! MY BEAUTY IS DANGEROUS!" AND THEN I SHOOT THE STARS AT THEM. . . . THAT'S BASICALLY, LIKE, MY THING WITH FASHION.

We did let you give a long explanation of your gi, Marco. So this is only fair.

Dress for Eternity: Choosing Your Outfit for the Blood Moon Ball

The Blood Moon Ball only happens once every 667 years, but let me tell ya, it's the event of the millennium.

If you live in the Underworld and like drinking punch that'll burn your face off.

Here's how to get into the Blood Moon Ball:

Cozy up to a demon. Or you can do what I did: dump a demon for being an angry rage monster jerky-jerk. He'll be back!

2. Use the creepy little ruby demon bell you get from your demon ex-boyfriend to summon a demon carriage.

3. When the demon carriage operator asks you which floor, always say "the bottom."

4. You can also crash the party like Marco did.

"Crash" is a strong word. It was more like "sneak into."

But what are you gonna wear? Ask yourself: Horns or no horns? Is red my best color? Does this cape make me look short? Can I take my wand or is that déclassé?

Here are Star Butterfly's
five tips for dressing down
for the Underworld:

1. **Stick to doing your own thing.** Don't wear
   any weird demon hair-things just to make
   yourself "blend in" with the crowd.

2. **Don't use magic on your face.** It hurts . . . and
   your face is awesome as it is.

3. **Choose the proper headgear.** Horns can be great,
   but if you're not feeling them, pull a Marco and
   wear what makes you comfortable.

4. I wore a charro costume, which is sort of a modern take on the old Mexican cowboy outfits. The one

I wore to the Blood Moon Ball was my dad's. He doesn't like me to wear it, because he thinks he will fit into it again. But what's a better way to hide your face around a bunch of demons than wearing a Día de los Muertos skull mask?

5. Make sure your outfit is blood-resistant. You never know when you're gonna have to take a prom pic while bathed in unicorn blood.

JUST PULL A B-FLY AND TELL 'EM UR BESTIE IS A UNICORN AND UR FACE IS A UNICORN-BLOOD-FREE ZONE.

6. Have fun. That's not really just a tip for this list, because you should have fun wherever you go!

HOW TO GET SMOKY EYES WHEN YOU'RE BEHIND BARS

OKAY, SO LIKE BEING LOCKED UP IN ST. O'S IS LIKE BASICALLY LITERALLY TERRIBLE, BUT U CAN STILL FEEL BEAUTIFUL OUTSIDE WHEN UR ON THE DIRTY INSIDE . . . OF ST. O'S.

Why are you always screaming?

SOME GIRLS ON THE INSIDE LET THEMSELVES GO, AND THAT JUST DOESN'T WORK FOR ME. ALSO, IF U LOOK TOO GOOD THEN IT'S LIKE UR A PUNK AND PEOPLE WILL TAKE UR LUNCH FROM YOU. I AIN'T NOBODY'S PUNK, BUT I STILL WANNA LOOK PUT TOGETHER, SO I LIKE TO ROCK SMOKY EYES.

HERE IS MY RECIPE FOR SMOKY EYES:

1. U WILL NEED A MAGICAL HORN OUT OF WHICH U CAN FIRE A LASER BEAM. IF U DO NOT HAVE A MAGICAL HORN, U WILL NOT BE ABLE TO ACHIEVE SMOKY EYES BEHIND BARS. I'M SORRY. U WILL LOOK BASIC.

2. FIND A SMALL PIECE OF WOOD.

3. LASER BEAM THE WOOD WITH YOUR HORN.

4. TAKE THE PILE OF BURNT WOOD AND DIP IT IN SOME UNICORN TEARS. IF U AREN'T A UNICORN, U WON'T BE ABLE TO DO THIS PART, SO U WILL JUST HAVE A PILE OF BURNT-UP WOOD AND YOU'LL PROBABLY BE LIKE, "WHY DIDN'T I JUST KEEP MY WOOD THE WAY IT WAS?" IT'S WHY U SHOULD READ ALL THE DIRECTIONS FIRST. STOP COMPLAINING.

5. ONCE U HAVE THIS BURNT-UP WOOD IN UR UNICORN TEARS, MAKE A MUD FROM IT AND PAINT IT ON UR EYEZ LIKE U OWN IT, KNOW WHAT I MEAN?

BEFORE — — — — — AFTER

Horns or Cacti: Making a Statement with Your Headgear

Everyone knows that your choice of headgear can say a lot about you. Like my red horns. I wear them all the time because they're my favorite. They tell the world that I'm fierce but fun. Wild, but I get things done. That I'm a leader, but I'm good at dancing.

How do they say that?

They just do, Marco. I don't know how. But sometimes a situation arises that calls for something different, when my red horns just aren't right. That's when I let my wand do the deciding.

Like when I was infiltrating St. Olga's Reform School for Wayward Princesses to save one of my besties.

EXCUZE ME . . . I WANT SOME ONCE-AND-FOR-ALL CLARIFICATION. . . . EARTHTURD IS YOUR SECOND BESTIE. RIGHT?

My wand decided that a pair of extra-long curved demon horns are a must when looking to do some serious undercover jailbreaking. The pale white ends of the horns are super shiny and tell the world that you mean business.

Match these scenarios with the appropriate headgear below:

1. You're invited to a birthday party in a restaurant that looks like an old ship.

2. A rival football team steals your school's mascot and you have to get into warrior mode to rescue it.

3. You're going on a school trip to the desert and you want to blend in with the scenery.

4. Princess Pony Head invites you on a staycation in the clouds with the whole Pony Head family.

5. There's a monster meet-up at the Botanical Gardens.

6. Magical pink wings appear on your back.

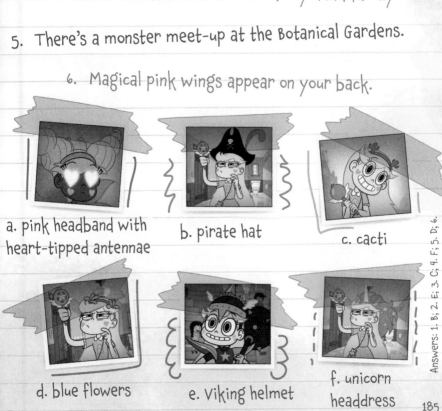

a. pink headband with heart-tipped antennae

b. pirate hat

c. cacti

d. blue flowers

e. Viking helmet

f. unicorn headdress

PONIES DON'T DO HEADGEAR

UNNECESSARY. SOME OF US ARE BLESSED WITH NATURAL HEADGEAR. LOOK, B-FLY, YOU CAN WEAR WHATEVER AND I WON'T JUDGE IT EVEN IF IT'S DUMB. BE AS DUMB AS YOU LIKE BECAUSE I LUV U. I SUPPORT THAT CUZ THAT'S WHAT BESTIES DO. BUT AS FAR AS HEADGEAR GOES, FOR ME, WELL, I DON'T WANNA INTERRUPT WHAT I LIKE TO CALL "THE PYRAMID OF INTEREST."

BASICALLY, IF YOU DRAW A LINE FROM THE TIP OF MY NATURAL HORN DOWN TO THE BOTTOM OF MY EARS AND ACROSS MY SMOKY EYES, IT MAKES A PYRAMID SHAPE.

Pyramids are three-dimensional.
I think you mean a triangle . . . just sayin'.

N.E.WAYZ, INSIDE OF THIS PYRAMID YOU WILL SEE THAT I AM BEAUTIFUL. PEEKABOO! IT'S ME. . . . BUT IF THIS PYRAMID IS BROKEN UP BY NOISY HEADGEAR, THEN IT DISTRACTS FROM MY BEAUTY. . . . NOT MUCH, OKAY . . . BUT I GO FROM LIKE A 10+ DOWN TO A 10 OR 9.9. NO THANK YOU.

Model 42 Z

$7.00
or
100 for $650.00

Jacket Phat's multi-position SLOUCH-A-HOOD* hoodie adjusts to fit every body type from teeny tiny to terrificallly tall, with rugged Zexxon* zipper technology that's easy on your fingers. Jacket Phat's hand-driven 24-inch Encircalator* helps provide triple-smooth closing power. Jacket Phat's hoodie . . . priced right at over 73 Kstart stores across the USA. Sale ends July 11. You really hood up!

*SLOUCH-A-HOOD, Zexxon & Encircalator are registered trademarks
of the Random Energy Corporation

The Happy Place

Copyright 2011   Kstart Corp.   Bakersfield 00001

What Your Cheek Emblems Say About You

Some people wear their hearts on their sleeves. I wear mine on my cheeks. It's something that's been in my family for ages; when you're around magic as much as we are, it leaves a mark. My mom, Queen Butterfly, has diamonds instead of hearts . . . and my great-great-great-great grandma Eclipsa (the one who married a monster) had spades.

> DON'T FORGET MISS HEINOUS. WHEN I WAS AT ST. O'S I SAW A PICTURE OF HER WHEN SHE WAS OUR AGE AND SHE HAD CLUBS ON HER CHEEKS!

But Heinous isn't part of the Butterfly family. . . . Ohhh . . . a <u>mystery</u>. I loooove mysteries.

My hearts have a mind of their own and sometimes, when I'm not paying attention, they do crazy things . . . like change into skulls or lightbulbs. *Lightbulbs = Bad idea.*

Cracked Heart:

When the bad stuff is at your back,
a cracked heart says things are out of whack.

B-FLY, YOU ARE A RHYMING FOOL!

Glowing Heart:

When you dip down deep to find the magic inside of you to help your friends.

Lightbulb:

Or not so great

Sometimes you get a great idea and your cheek emblems can't help getting involved.

Skull with Heart Eyes:

When you may or may not have booby-trapped an entire football field to protect your school's football team.

Not a big fan of the Kitty Cat Offense ... and giant monster squirrels aren't great, either.

Spinning Hourglass:

Boredom. The very foe this book seeks to vanquish. Sometimes you can't help using your cheek emblems to show how bored you are.

The Wand: Heirloom, Weapon, Accessory—and It Tastes Great! (Nom, Nom, Nom)

When I turned fourteen, I inherited the Royal Magic Wand from my mom, the queen. It's been handed down this way, queen to firstborn princess, for as long as anyone can remember.

The cool thing about it is that the wand takes on the personality of whoever holds it, so it's always in style! Imagine I had to drag around some musty old grandma wand. No thanks.

Remember when your wand grew claws?

You mean when you were trying to make Lobster Claws become good, when deep down he was a monster . . . and monsters don't want to be good?

Oh, yeah, I forgot that part.

Basic Wand Anatomy

My wand is basically like most wands. It has a **grip** where you hold it, a **bell**, and a **crystal**. At the base of the grip is the **charge port**, which is where you connect the **wand charger**.

The Crystal
The crystal focuses the spell, once you've cast it.

The Bell
The bell is the most delicious part of the wand (mine tastes like caramel corn) and it is where the wand core is housed. Basically, anyone who has ever held the wand infuses their experiences with it into the wand core. It also houses the mill.

The Mill
The inside of a wand is a crazy no-man's land of memories, spirits, and a Millhorse. There's a tiny mill inside the wand that grinds the sapphire crystals from the charger, and the Millhorse runs the mill. If the wand is low on crystals, the mill has nothing to grind, so the Millhorse runs himself ragged. It's sad when that happens, so keep your wand charged!

You blew up your first wand.

Yeah . . . I wasn't gonna mention that, but okay, yeah, it's different now. It used to be cute—all lavender and gold with sparkles and fluffy wings—but then I had to destroy my wand to save Marco from getting smushed, and when I destroyed it, it didn't really destroy. . . . It kinda came back.

Is it the same wand?

I'm actually not sure. It feels the same but different, ya know? Like an old friend with a new look. Sometimes my spells don't come out quite as I'd expect, or if I'm . . . uh . . . distracted or just not in a good head space . . . my wand is kinda funky.

The Charge Port and Wand Charger
Wands have to be charged with magical energy by connecting a charger to the charge port about once every year or so. The charger feeds microscopic crystals into the wand. All wands are different, but my wand drinks mystic sapphire crystals.

Speaking of wand, I wand something to eat. Let's end this thing.

Huh?

I wand-ta stop writing the book now. Say g'night, Marco!

Wait . . . Star . . . this is NOT how you end a book. The end of a book is something you sorta want to ease your audience into; the end can be tearful, maybe even heartbreaking.

Say whatever you want—I'll be in the kitchen! G'night, everybody!

Okay . . . well, dear reader, I guess this is farewell. I know it's sad it's over, but I won't leave you without a remedy for the pain of the End of the Book. Here's my favorite recipe for finishing a book.

BOOK END RECIPE
1 Box generic facial tissues
1 Pint Choclin' Dobbs Chocolate Peanut Butter Ice Cream (or similar)
1 Bottle Cow-nt Down to Sundae Chocolate Sauce (or similar)
1 Pillow (or 2, to taste) EWW. MARCO, YOUR RECIPE MAKES ME UNCOMFORTABLE. OK, BYEEEEE!!!

Before you get to the End of the Book (like what you're reading right now), lie on your stomach, bunching the pillow under your chest, supporting your chin. Wrap your arms around the pillow, holding the book open in front of you. As you approach the Final Sentence*, make sure the tissues are within reach, and then cry freely as you read.

After the book is closed, drizzle the Cow-nt Down to Sundae Chocolate Sauce over the Choclin' Dobbs Chocolate Peanut Butter Ice Cream, and ladle it generously into your crying mouth. At this point it is traditional to let the tears stream down the sides of your face as you eat.

It's not unusual to fall asleep in your tears and melted ice cream.

*This is the Final Sentence. NO, THIS IS!

MARCO-PO-PARCO!!!!

Hey! I'm writing this letter and I'm so excited that my dad is going to let me use his RAZOR CRANE to deliver it! They have beaks that can cut dimensional rifts!

Anyway, I'm home on Mewni for this boring conference. A lot of people with beards and/or horns and/or gills sitting

at a big table, arguing about boundaries and the future . . . and no magic allowed in the room, so I can't even take my compact and play Gem Mania. :(

I brought our book with me and it was so much fun to open it and see all the pictures and the funny stuff. . . . I had NO IDEA that you did all those steps to make nachos for me, Marco. I might do magic, but if you ask me, that recipe is some other kinda magic.

Okay, I gotta go now but I'll see you soon. P.S. Can you water my cactus headband for me? He gets three drops at the end of the week.

Star